Michigan Quarterly Review

Vol. XXXIV, No. 3   Summer 1995

MICHIGAN QUARTERLY REVIEW (ISSN 0026–2420) is published quarterly (January, April, July, and October) by The University of Michigan, Rm 3032 Rachham Bldg., 915 E. Washington St., Ann Arbor, MI 48109–1070. Subscription prices, $18.00 a year, $36.00 for two years; Institutional subscriptions obtained through agencies $20.00 a year; $5.00 a copy; back issues, $2.50. Claims for missing numbers can be honored only within two months after publication.

Available on microfilm from Xerox University Microfilms, 300 N. Zeeb Rd., Ann Arbor, Michigan 48106, where full-sized copies of single articles may also be ordered. Reprinted volumes and back-volumes available from AMS Press, Inc., 56 E. 13th St., New York, 10003. Indexed or abstracted in Abstr.E.S., Am.Bib.Cent., Ann.Bib., Bk.R.Hum, BK.R.Inc., P.A.I.S.,P.M.L.A., Index of American Periodical Verse, Index to Periodical Fiction, American Humanities Index.

Editorial and business office, 3032 Rackham Bldg., The University of Michigan, Ann Arbor, Michigan 48109. Unsolicited manuscripts are returned to authors only when accompanied by stamped, self-addressed envelopes or by international postal orders. No responsibility assumed for loss or injury.

Second class postage paid at Ann Arbor, Michigan. Send address changes to *Michigan Quarterly Review*, Rm 3032 Rackham Bldg., 915 E. Washington St., Ann Arbor, MI 48109–1070.

TO OUR READERS

Michigan Quarterly Review is now offering a complete index of all issues dating back to the first in 1962. The index, alphabetized by author, was prepared this year by Bich Nguyen, and will be kept current. It is available on computer disk (not on paper), on 3.5 inch MS Word for Windows or 3.5 inch MS Word 5 for Macintosh.

To order, send a check for $5.00 to: *Michigan Quarterly Review*, 3032 Rackham Bldg., University of Michigan, Ann Arbor, MI 48109–1070.

CONTENTS

Cover: Paul Touvier, on the first day of trial
March 17, 1994
Courtesy *Le Progrès*

CONTRIBUTORS

ALICE ADAMS's most recent novel was *Almost Perfect*; her forthcoming novel, *Exposure*, also from Alfred A. Knopf, will be published next season.

S. BEN-TOV's first book of poetry was *During Ceasefire*, from Harper & Row; and she is publishing this season a work of literary history, *The Artful Paradise: Science Fiction and American Reality* (University of Michigan Press). She is Assistant Professor of English at Bowling Green State University.

SARAH CHAYES covered the trial of Paul Touvier for Monitor Radio; she is Monitor Radio's chief Paris correspondent. She has published essays and reportage in *The New York Times*, *The Christian Science Monitor, Reconstruction*, and elsewhere.

TEMMA EHRENFELD has worked for *Fortune, Life,* and the *Washington Post* syndicate. This is her second appearance in MQR.

ROBERT FEKETY is on retirement furlough from the Medical School of the University of Michigan, where he served as Professor of Internal Medicine and Chief, Division of Infectious Diseases.

PAUL FRANKS is a junior member of the Society of Fellows, and teaches in the philosophy department, at the University of Michigan. He received his Ph.D. from Harvard in 1993, and is now revising his dissertation, *Why is Hegel So Hard to Understand? The Transformation of Philosophical Esotericism from Kant to Hegel.*

EMILY HIESTAND's books are *Green the Witch-Hazel Wood* (poetry, Graywolf, 1989) and *The Very Rich Hours* (travel essays, Beacon, 1992). Forthcoming are *Alluvial* (poetry) and *Travels at Home* (essays, Beacon Press). Trained as a painter, her recent visual artworks combine paintings, words, and photographic images.

DIANE JOHNSON's most recent novels are *Persian Nights* (1987) and *Health and Happiness* (1990), both from Alfred A. Knopf. A distinguished literary critic, she also published in 1992 a volume of travel essays, *Natural Opium*. She is the author of a biography of Dashiell Hammett, and of the screenplay for *The Shining*.

LAURA KASISCHKE's first collection of poems, *Wild Brides*, was published by New York University Press. A new collection, *Housekeeping in a Dream*, appeared last season from Carnegie Mellon University Press.

F. D. REEVE is Secretary of New York's Poets House and the founder a dozen years ago of *Poetry Review*. He is the author of *Concrete Music*, the recent *A Few Rounds of Old Maid and Other Stories*, and a book of poems coming next spring, *The Blue Boat on the St.. Anne*.

ENRICO MARIO SANTÍ, Professor of Latin American Literature at Georgetown University, has been named the 1996 Emilio Bacardi Moreau Professor of Cuban Studies at The University of Miami, Coral Gables. In addition to his books on Pablo Neruda and Octavio Paz, he is the author of *Pensar a Jose Martí* and *Por una politeratura*, both forthcoming this year.

ABBE SMITH is Deputy Director and Clinical Instructor, Criminal Justice Institute, Harvard Law School, and Lecturer on Law, Trial Advocacy Workshop, Harvard Law School. She received her B.A. from Yale in 1978 and her J.D. in 1982 from New York University School of Law.

ILAN STAVANS, a novelist and critic, teaches at Amherst College. His most recent books are *The Hispanic Condition* and *Bandido* (both HarperCollins). *The Invention of Memory and Other Stories* is forthcoming from University of New Mexico Press. His biographical essay on Gabriel García Márquez appeared in the Spring 1995 issue of MQR.

STEVE YARBROUGH is the author of the short story collections *Family Men* (LSU Press, 1990) and *Mississippi History* (University of Missouri, 1994). He teaches at California State University, Fresno.

ARIEL DORFMAN
Photo by Jay Thompson

ILAN STAVANS

THE GRINGO'S TONGUE:
A CONVERSATION WITH ARIEL DORFMAN

Ariel Dorfman (b. 1942), responsible for, among other works, *Widows*, *The Last Song of Manuel Sendero*, *Death and the Maiden*, and *Konfidenz*, is a proud member of what could be called the "Translingual Literary Club," also populated by Joseph Conrad, Vladimir Nabokov, Jerzy Kosinski, Shmuel Yosef Agnon, and Franz Kafka, writers who consciously, and sometimes as a result of political circumstances, switched from one language to another to shape their creative oeuvre. Their linguistic odyssey is often marked by a sense of uprootedness, of lack of belonging. They write in what one might describe as "borrowed words." I first met Dorfman in Durham, North Carolina, at a translator's conference he organized at Duke University in October 1994, in which translators from north and south of the Rio Grande shared their notes on the craft. We began a friendly dialogue about polyglotism, memory, Judaism, and bicultural identities that continues to this day. The following interview, devoted to these issues, took place in March, 1995.

*   *   *   *

IS: Would you please map for me your transition from Spanish to English: what each of these languages means to you?
AD: I have spent my entire life switching languages. The book I am presently starting to write, a memoir, deals with this phenomenon. It's an attempt at a self-portrait that would also be a portrait of the world I've been crossing or traversing since I was very little. I was born in Buenos Aires, Argentina, but at two-and-a-half years of age I moved with my family to New York, where I had a traumatic experience. I contracted pneumonia. I entered the hospital speaking Spanish but when I came out I didn't speak a word of it. And I

wouldn't do so for another ten years. So my first language was Spanish, but I erased it in relation to speaking it, although I could still understand. I understood everything my parents would say to me, but I would answer them in English. Then, for complicated reasons, when I was twelve we went back to Latin America — more specifically to Chile, where I had to relearn Spanish. Soon I became enraptured with it, until 1968, when I went to Berkeley. At that point I was entirely bilingual. I had kept on writing in English while in Chile, but I had also begun writing essays in Spanish. By then I had already produced a book or two. At Berkeley I was a research scholar, and it was there I realized that everything I was writing about in fiction concerned my Latin American experience — the experience of the marginal, of the underdeveloped. Around that time I made a commitment to myself never again to write in English — a foolish proposal no doubt.

I then returned to Chile (it was the early seventies, an explosive revolutionary time in Latin America, when Salvador Allende had just come to power) and I swore that henceforth I would write only in Spanish. As I saw it, I had readopted, or had been readopted by, the Spanish language. But the gods of the twentieth century decided to play the cards differently. I went into exile at the end of 1973 and continued to write most of my fiction in Spanish, in exile, far from Chile. I spent some years in Paris and in Holland, and in 1980 my family and I came to the United States, supposedly for a very short period. We got stranded here, and the stranding meant that I had to make a living writing in English. I had to support my kids, I had to begin a new life. As time went by, very gradually — and this is where I find myself at the moment — I began to accept the fact of my bicultural, bilingual, split life . . . and the split languages that I inhabit, or that inhabit me. I ceased to be at odds with my binary identity. I ceased to fight. I'm currently finishing a BBC project (a screenplay) in English, I'm working on a play in Spanish, and I have the memoir I was telling you about, which will probably be in both tongues. I'm also thinking of a novel that will have one chapter in Spanish and one in English.

is: Talk to me a bit more about that novel. By writing it in both languages, you must necessarily be visualizing a bilingual reader, one as fluent in them as you are. But is there such an audience out there, one big enough for the publisher to be ready to embark on a risky project like this? Or are you only writing it in that way and the alternative chapters will then be translated into the other language? AD: An intriguing question. I'm only writing it that way in order to express myself the way I want to. *Mascara*, published in 1988, is the first of my novels that I wrote in Spanish, then rewrote in English, only to then use what I had redone in English to change the Spanish version. I had an editor at Viking who would work at the English text, and then I would change the Spanish accordingly. I did that because, as you Ilan know very well, there are very few editors in Latin America: your book undergoes little change between the time you submit it and the finished text. Once again, in this new novel I will do the translation myself. It will probably be a monolingual text written by a bilingual writer. But the issue of an audience ad hoc to my needs concerns me deeply. For me the perfect audience would be one made of some forty to sixty million people as bilingual as I am. I honestly think that if I had that audience I would write in an entirely different way. I would write the way I live: switching languages, going in and out, like the Nuyoricans and Chicanos. When you come to our house, you realize that first we say things in Spanish and then switch to English; we mix everything up. But then, when I'm in the world, a world organized categorically in a Kantian fashion, a world in which languages organize societies and create wars, one must acquire or perhaps call on a different self. Although I have never written a book with a specific market in mind, I do take into account whether somebody is going to read my text or not, whether someone is going to understand it or not. By the way, in my new novel I may create a landscape in which I have an entirely bilingual country.

IS: Henry James once tried to describe the difference between the first, original tongue, and its counterpart, the second, acquired one. He called the first the mother tongue and the second the wife or mistress tongue. It was a logical approach: James happened to be addressing someone who had English as a second tongue and he said, memorably, that English behaves like a mistress — it will be loyal to you if you take care of her, but it will betray you, be angry and offensive, if you misbehave. Taking that as a starting point, could you describe what Spanish means to you and likewise English? How do they behave toward you and you toward them? Which one would you rather have in an intimate moment? Which is the language of fury and which the language of dreams?

AD: Gosh, I wish I knew the answer. The fact that Henry James would talk about mistresses and wives is already a very gendered approach to the issue. Personally I'm not surprised that he would put it in those terms. In my own case, I really don't know which one came first, which one is nearest to me. One is the mother tongue in the sense that it's the language my mother spoke to me when I was a baby. But I have no memories of it. The language of my childhood, the language I chose, perhaps as an act of rebellion, is English. Spanish very slowly became the language of my maturation; it also became the language of love because it's the tongue in which I fell in love with Angélica, my wife. (Coincidentally, she was an English teacher when I met her.) In a way, I think I'm married to both languages, but marriage implies divorce and separation. Perhaps I have two mothers: two origins, two beginnings. Or is it two mother-wives? This does not preclude the fact that oftentimes I feel as if I don't have a language at all — a sort of aphasia: I can stumble, lose my sense of what language I'm using, and not find a word in either tongue; I can search for the word but the word is not there. Probably the deepest side of myself inhabits that no-language geography. When I'm writing, if the voice, the inner voice, comes to me in one language, I will follow through: I let the language choose me. By the way, languages in my life have never been neutral or apolitical. They often put me in awkward positions. During the seventies and the early eighties, I would find myself enjoying English, and I felt closest to it, even when English was the language of empire, the language of aggression and oppression. In spite of the fact that the language of Shakespeare, Jane Austen, and Humphrey Bogart, a *gringo* tongue (even if I spoke it better than the *gringos*) was often understood as an enemy language, I felt closer to it. This makes me think of Rubén Darío's admonition: *Vamos a rezar en inglés* — we will pray in English.

IS: Did that create guilt?

AD: I think so, for a large part of my life. Remember that I was born into a very well-to-do family by Chilean standards, and I would try to hide that fact. I kept on saying to myself: I should be writing in Spanish, because Spanish is the language of identity, the language of community shared by millions of people with whom I'm creating a New World, I'm dreaming the Revolution, and I'm dreaming the return to Democracy. Once settled in the U.S., I told myself: You are using English to help others understand Latin America, to analyze the many contradictions of the region, to explore the vicissitudes of Latin American intellectuals. But then I began to recognize that, deep inside myself, I always felt a bit of a stranger in Spanish. I'm not embarrassed by that anymore. Nowadays I don't try to hide my social background: I am who I am, and it's because of who I am that I can write the way I write. I don't see my bilingualism as a curse anymore. I've lived outside Chile for over two decades already and am accustomed to the linguistic dilemmas we've been talking about—they aren't new for me.

IS: Incidentally, I once talked to Oscar Hijuelos about the same topic. He isn't fully bilingual: his Spanish language is in his unconscious, in the background. He told me that the disappearance of his Spanish tongue took place at a very early age, when he entered a hospital for a few months to recover from a very serious sickness. The hospital was in New York and he soon discovered that unless he requested whatever he needed in English, the nurse practitioner wasn't going to do things his way. Just like you, he entered speaking Spanish and left speaking English. What's curious, I think, is that both of you lost, or found, a tongue in a hospital. A hospital, a sickness and a recovery—these were the ingredients.

AD: Extraordinary. As for me, I can't remember a single thing that happened in that hospital. Not a single thing. Everything has been erased from memory.

IS: I have in front of me the two versions of *Konfidenz*, Spanish and English. As you know, often when a text is translated from Spanish to English, the resulting text is smaller in size—in pages. But in your book there's only one page difference: 175 and 176, which seems to me incredible. As writers we often need to further explain, or substantially delete, segments of the text for a translation to be successful. We are addressing a different audience, with different cultural needs. But if length is any indication, you have achieved a perfect balance. Balance of syntax and grammar. Balance of content. Balance of cultures. You add and take in the same proportion.

AD: I began to try solving the problems of exile by writing simultaneously for an audience back home and for one abroad. By doing so, I was hoping that words would become the meeting ground of what was within and without, outside and inside. The text was the in-between, a fusion, an amalgamation, signifying in one way and in the other depending on who was reading. Likewise, my characters have a tendency, though grounded in a certain reality, to become ghosts — to signify other realities. *Death and the Maiden* takes place in a country that could be Chile (it's probably Chile), but that can also be any place in Africa, in the Middle East, in Eastern Europe under the same circumstance. The same with *Konfidenz*, which makes the reader think it's about Latin America, although in fact it's about Nazis, Jews, and the resistance during World War II. I started doing this with *Widows*, which, although it's about the *desapareci-dos* in Argentina, is set in Greece, and to do so I created a pseudony-mous Danish author, who is supposedly the one writing the whole story. A very Latin America idea, I should add, harking back to Borges, Julio Cortázar, Alejo Carpentier, and even Pablo Neruda: we're all echoes, shadows of something original and originary, hand-me-downs, residuals, anticipations of something utopian still to appear.

IS: Was *Death and the Maiden* written in Spanish?

AD: Yes, and then I almost immediately and very feverishly trans-lated it into English.

IS: Spinoza wrote *Ethics* in Latin but thought it in Hebrew. And one could say something similar about Kafka's German, if not about Nabokov's English and French. Could you describe your Spanish to me? Soon after I left Mexico, my editors back home began to com-plain that the columns and stories I would send from New York were written in Spanish but thought out in English. And my Spanish today, well . . . it's bookish, abstract, alien, foreign, anything but regional.

AD: Likewise with me: my Spanish is haunted by English, and vice versa. People in Latin America react toward my Spanish by saying, we don't know where you fit. Consequently, and like you, I'm drawn to bilingual writers, certainly the ones you mentioned or those that sound bilingual. I used to feel uncomfortable because I didn't belong, but now I'm happy to be loyal to my calling.

IS: Yours, then, is a written English with a Spanish accent.

AD: Yes. For instance, when I write for the *New York Times* an editor may suggest changing an adjective to make the sentence correct. But I fight with my life against it. I want to write for the *gringo* with a sense of familiarity. After all, I'm also a *gringo*. I was brought up in this country, and I know what it means and feels to be a U.S. citizen. But I also want to convey in my writing a sense of aliena-tion, distance, discomfort. I will fight against stubborn editors to retain my own syntax, my own voice. Maybe I'm trying to be true *and* translated simultaneously.

IS: Bilingual writers, writers fully active in two or more languages, might have an internalized translator. It makes it easier for editors to come directly to us, since at least one intermediary — the translator — is unneeded. You are your own translator. So in the old saying, *traduttore traditore*, the only one guilty here is oneself. On the other hand, translators are the closest to a perfect reader one can ever dream of having. They know the dirty tricks, the subterfuges, the many masks a writer has. A translator can bring out the best in a writer and also the worst. As I think you will agree, often a translation improves the original — the second reader, the perfect reader, elevates the text to a higher standard. But by being your own translator (and here I of course also talk of myself), we are miserably deprived of that gift. We are deprived of the dialogue one can have with one's best possible reader.

AD: I couldn't agree with you more. It's a wonderful observation. You do miss a step. One of the problems one has as a writer is that you tend to fall in love with your own language, with your own words. When you yourself translate them, I think you tend to be literal and, thus, you miss that step: in a sense, what you miss is to be betrayed. But there's a positive and a negative aspect to betrayal. On the one hand, it can be the worst possible fate for a work of art, and not capriciously did Dante place traitors at the heart of hell. I myself think loyalty is the most important of all human qualities. On the other hand, as I've experienced life, I realize that there are moments of let's call it good betrayal. Moments when you have to leave yourself, the past, and certain people behind in order to grow. You have to cross a border at a certain point and turn your back on a few things. Pure loyalty is also a loss of self. You give yourself entirely to someone else, so you may not know who you are. I don't know if I have a translator inside: the two languages inhabiting me are contiguous, as if there's a customs office between them. I go back and forth — as if I had simultaneously two faces, which I could switch on and off.

IS: You come from a Jewish family. I wonder if there were other tongues aside from English and Spanish — French or Yiddish, perhaps. Also, I wonder if the environment in which you grew up championed polyglotism. You already told me how you would talk to your parents in English and they would respond in Spanish. . . .

AD: I began thinking about all these things only recently. For instance, I have realized, while writing my memoir, that both of my parents were bilingual. That is, I knew it all along but in the past few months the fact has acquired new importance. My father was born in Russia and Russian was his first language. He stills speaks it perfectly. He's trilingual: English, Spanish, and Russian. Both he and my mother also speak a little bit of French. And my mother was brought up with Yiddish — her first language — because she was born in Romania, and at three months old she left for Buenos Aires. She still speaks some Yiddish and understands some German. Obviously my maternal grandparents spoke Yiddish, and my paternal ones spoke Russian. Thus, my two parents had the experience of acquiring a second language. All this is to say that, you're right Ilan, my childhood milieu was multilingual but, also, as I told you before, that having two languages at times felt like having a birthmark on my childhood face — an invisible, yet painful birthmark. Now I realize that it was also exhilarating.

IS: We've been talking about translation and polyglotism, about memory, suffering and justice. Would you consider yourself, now more than before, a Jewish writer? Of course a Jewish writer is a person that is Jewish and that writes. But I would like to go further. You've discussed Kafka's influence on you and betrayal of a certain past and a certain pattern as a strategy to move onward with life. Every Jewish writer is a hybrid: a transnational, transgenerational, transcultural, and translingual entity, one that goes places but has no specific address, and has influences that come from far beyond his immediate milieu, and often his work cannot find an echo in that milieu. Considering your own present ambivalence toward Chile — when I saw you last, you told me you couldn't live in Chile any longer — I wonder how you feel about "the Jewish question."

AD: I have changed in this regard. For most of my life I thought I was Jewish merely by accident, that I was Latin American by choice, and that it had befallen on me to be an English-speaking person. Let me stress it once more: my identity was centrally that of Latin America, which I defined as a resistant Latin America and a revolutionary Latin America. I perceived the region as eternally hopeful, in a permanent journey toward a better future, toward a Promised Land. But as years go by, I feel I belong but that I also don't belong. No matter how much I drink of Latin America, I'm never full, I'm always missing something in my relationship toward the continent, both as I see it and as the region sees me or avoids seeing me. Consequently, already for some time I have begun defining myself as a Latin American who is everywhere and nowhere. I feel at home in many places and, to be perfectly honest, I like and feel comfortable with my wandering condition. Often I'm struck by nostalgia and sadness, by the realization that I will always be globe-trotting, that I will never call a piece of land my own. I think that's my destiny, an anticipatory and prophetic destiny in the sense that I know I'm participating in a new breed of humanity, a cross-national breed. When I begin to define myself in these abstract terms, I realize that by definition I'm as old as my ancestors — that is, I'm Jewish. If for decades I thought of Jews simply as being very much the observers of a series of religious habits and I observe none of these (my mother was brought up in a Zionist household and my father was very much an agnostic who rejected the very idea of Judaism and fought for world revolution), now I've discovered I might be Jewish in the deepest sense. After all, I'm messianic, pro-foundly (perhaps perversely) ethical; like a Talmudist I discover multiple readings in every text. Recently I went to the Jewish Museum in New York and was mesmerized by photos and images of the *shtetl*, which I felt were looking at me, not only the other way around. Some eyes in those photos were my eyes, calling to me from inside my past. So there you find me, Ilan: while I used to answer that I'd be Jewish until the day when there was no more anti-Semitism, today I'm more conscious of my background. Jewish characters have appeared in my work: in *The Last Song of Manuel Sendero*, for instance, David, one of the protagonists (which happens to have been the name of both my grandfathers), is an eternal wanderer; and Judaism and Nazism are at the center of *Konfidenz*. I must add to all this that I never experience an excessive amount of anti-Semitism in Chile, not from the Left and not even under Pinochet. Unlike dictators in Argentina like Perón and the tyrants of the Dirty War, Augusto Pinochet was not an anti-Semite.

is: Why was *Death and the Maiden* so successful in Israel?

ad: I have heard that it is a magnificent production. But its success may also be due to its literary structure. The play is deliberately written to allow different audiences to read into it their own dilemmas, allegorically speaking. It is something of a deformed mirror, and, as you remember, a mirror appears at the very end. If the public, collectively speaking, is worried about the problems on stage (justice, evil, memory, how one tells one's own tragic story so that it's confirmed by others, and what happens if one suddenly ceases to be marginal and acquires enormous power which can be exercised against a former enemy), then it will be attracted to my characters and their questions. As you know, the play was very successful on Broadway, but it was successful in monetary and artistic terms, not in engaging the community to ask questions about itself. It had fine actors and was sold out for six months. But as with the movie adaptation directed by Roman Polanski, no one wrote an op-ed piece saying, "Here's a set of questions affecting us deeply, which we should address." People saw it as one more play or motion picture. It was different in the cases of Israel, Belgrade, Belfast, Brazil, Kenya. Audiences were able to read their own experiences into the text. In Israel in particular, what people saw on stage was not the Latin American but the Jewish and the Israeli experience. As a people, Jews have been about as deeply hurt as one can possibly be in this world — in relation to persecution, damage, and destruction brought upon us. I believe that anybody who is Jewish has to ask himself whether to pardon those who committed atrocities against us — especially today, as anti-Semitism, ethnic violence and chauvinism rear their head again. Also, the three characters in *Death and the Maiden* could be Palestinian . . . and that was an issue I discussed with the Israeli director when the play was in rehearsal. Israel, then, probably used Chile as mirror and so did Germany, which, by the way, is where my play has been most successful — 64 different productions at this point, I think. Perhaps Germans are also exploring their guilt — their multiple pasts.

DIANE JOHNSON

THE WRITER AS A CHARACTER

It's a particular pleasure to be here, because Ann Arbor has always been a place of legend to me. I am the sister and daughter of University of Michigan alumni, but I have never visited the campus. Over the years I have had several friends who received Hopwood prizes — a few days ago I had lunch with Edmund White, my neighbor in Paris. I don't know when I have read a book as avidly as Nicholas Delbanco's anthology of former Hopwood lectures, *Speaking of Writing*. Writers in America, dispersed as we are, starve for shoptalk, and this collection is like having a wonderful conversation about literature with an impressive and admired group of predecessors on this podium.

When I was done reading it, I had a lot of "how true's" in the margin, not to mention "but ifs." I might have taken as my text Norman Mailer's observation that "Experience when it cannot be communicated to another must wither within and be worse than lost." How true, though maybe only true for writers? That is, for people who must write, as compared to people who want to lead a writer's life. Creative writing classes are full of both types, often equally talented; but the latter usually don't end up being writers, perhaps because they don't have the writer's sort of character. My subject I could describe as being the writer's character as desired by the reader, and revealed in the old-fashioned elements of the narrative — plot, style, and subject — coincidentally the very narrative elements Saul Bellow said in his Hopwood lecture of 1961 were finished. Bellow especially attacked "the badly faded ideas of motives and drama or love and hate" as being possibly only of interest to clinical psychologists and sociologists. That was very much in the Freud-dominated spirit of the time, and things were to get worse

The Hopwood Lecture, 1995

for the old-fashioned art of story-telling, which I would like to offer a little defense of today.

By chance, on my way here, something happened that exactly illustrates my theme. I was in the airport bookshop. It might as well have been called the Danielle Steele bookshop, completely lined from floor to ceiling and wall to wall with books by this popular author. A woman wondering at the vast array of alluring titles asked the bookshop lady "but which one?" "Oh, it doesn't matter," said the bookstore lady. "They're all Steeles." This in turn reminded me of a few years ago, when I was one of several writers on a program, one of whom was Louis L' Amour, the writer of western novels, with an audience of four thousand attentive listeners who to a person lined up afterward to get L' Amour's signature on their old copies of his books. Yet, I now discover, few readers can mention the titles or any of the characters or recount the plots of L' Amour's or Steele's novels, let alone quote a line. The qualities that drew these readers were inherent in the writers, not in the works, some resonance of sensibility.

I wish I could announce that I was here going to reveal the secret of selling millions of copies of novels. Alas. But I do want to say something about the neglected subject of the writer herself, himself, in his pages, carrying over from book to book. The author, not the narrator. I mean the sense we have as we read there are three of us involved — ourself, the narrator, and the writer. Reading *Huckleberry Finn*, there are Huck and I, and Mark Twain, and as I read, I address certain thoughts to Twain, no matter how scarce he makes himself, hiding behind Huck. As readers I think we always have a sense of an author's presence, alive in her text, looking over our shoulder as we read, and we have an affection for one author over another; and there's the fact that though we will read about characters we don't like, we don't read a writer whom we don't like. The practical implication of this for us as writers is that it is ourselves, finally, that have to stand up to some serious tests of not only talent and industry but character, commitment, and what Henry James called, rather dauntingly, "quality of mind."

I should say again that I'm talking about the writer as distinct from the narrator. In an allegory painting of narrative fiction, the narrator would be the Madonna or saint in the middle of the picture, and the writer would be the God-like figure behind, up in the sky, with golden rays of force emitting from his forehead or fingers.

There is of course one thing particularly medieval and naive about the painting—the unfashionable figure of God. God is not represented in modern painting, just as the writer is no longer admitted into his narrative except as subject. It is in part the direction all art has gone, from naive allegory to abstract expressionism. Flaubert decreed that the author should be "nowhere apparent." Roland Barthes in 1968 took a harder line; as an "institution the author is dead." The irrelevance of the writer to the literary project, the death of the writer, was announced somewhat after the death of God, but the two demises are not unrelated, I think, and are part of a general modern political dynamic, pushing from the left to devalue or challenge authority of any kind, terrorizing on the right with death threats for authorial transgressions.

Serious critics from Michigan or Yale have by now abandoned speaking of the writer at all. Once he has performed his unwitting creative part, we are told to forget about him and his intentions in the work, his need for money in the winter of 1942, his lifelong obsession for frogs—the text must stand for itself. The worst of this is that writers have tended to accept the death of the writer too. I think as American writers we have shrunk from our readers. This may sound odd in a time when people write about themselves obsessively, with a kind of unstoppable reflex candor—we are so good at "sharing" our feelings. Europeans say American friendliness is our disguise, our candor a mask behind which, because we omit knowable social rites, we are unknowable. The first-person, with its confidential, natural tone and indifference to plot, can mask us and distract us.

I think, and now I speak as a reader, that the reader must have a sense of the writer there, that dialogue is implicit in art. Even Barthes, having dismissed him, later goes on to admit that in the text we "desire the author; [we] need his figure . . . as he needs [ours]." Just as every writer has an invisible, minatory reader dimly in mind, who says things like "she would never do that," or even, "don't put in so much description, can't you get along with the story faster?" the reader, for his part, has an invisible but tangible writer in mind to whom he says "how true" or "but if." Where there is no author, as in the case of oral literature or anonymous works, we tend either to invent him (never her, e.g., "Homer") or attribute the work to someone who does or did exist. Shakespeare is almost the oddest case, an author of such genius that he cannot have existed—I speak of the attempts to question his identity or ascribe his works to others. The easy appeal of the too autobiographical first-person narrative, however, can impede dialogue because one cannot challenge narrative elements compelled less by art than by circumstance.

I think a reader sees a writer as vividly as in a painting and we modify our image of him as a part of reading. We might see D. H. Lawrence wearing a lascivious smile until we realize he is kind of a prude whose inclusion of sexually explicit passages is the reflex of his discomfort with the whole subject of sex. Now we put a scowl on his face, rather like the scowl on the face of Carlyle. Dickens is fat. My own image of Twain comes from my childhood game of Authors. However you get it, this image changes according to the information you have, inferred from the attitudes, subject matter, and even mistakes we find in a book, and also what you might know of the author's real life. Our ideas about the writer may have come from that curious genre the literary biography. Why actually would one want to read about Wallace Stevens or Henry Green—the lives of most writers aren't very interesting—except to influence and clarify our malleable and developing image of a writer whose works we cherish, very much as we update the picture we have of our friends. We miss the author photo on the jacket if it isn't there. I have to tell you that when those four thousand people lined up before Louis L' Amour, clutching worn, beloved copies of his books, he refused to sign the paperbacks, only the hardbacks, and I've always wondered if those rejected readers went on reading him with as much affection as before.

I am not saying that the reader thus imposes a responsibility on you the writer in your daily life, to be a moral force or public figure. It may be that he tries, but I'm not talking at all about the writer's material self, his personality in the world, his media side. Let us pass over that. Writers like celebrity as much as the next person, but it never seems to have helped anyone write. Lionizing is not just a malady of the modern world—people have always seized upon writers if they are glamorous. They rarely are. We have all seen those spreads in *People*, say, the homely, ordinary-looking writer in his study, usually with some touching affectation of dress, say cowboy boots or a big hat, by which he hopes to set himself apart. Byron, or Marlowe, or Hemingway had glamour, but it is not given to most writers, nor to most mortals in any profession, not even for fifteen minutes. And most of us manage to avoid feeling too much regret about that. I should acknowledge that Louis L' Amour did not disappoint in glamour; he was a white-haired old man like the figure of God, and wore a great array of turquoise jewelry and a fringed buckskin jacket.

The you in your text is not the same as you the living person. I was recently in Saudi Arabia, where women, even western women, are obliged to wear a kind of black choir-robe, called the abbaya, and a black head covering which is pulled across the face, rendering you invisible, though you can see, rather imperfectly, through the semi-transparent fabric. Once invisible, I found myself to change, my personality changed. If I am, as I imagine, usually, reserved and polite, I became assertive and frank as I try to be in print. As I stood with a group of men at the hotel elevator, and they piled in and allowed the doors to close behind them without me, from beneath my veil I heard my own voice loudly and rudely denounce them as a bunch of jerks. Incidentally I should say that I felt that the veil, though symbolically odious, has this same liberating function for women in Islamic societies, in that it gives them license to speak without gender, and this is why they put up with it. About gender, I myself think the writer's persona has no particular sex in the text. The disadvantages of being a writer who is a woman are all external — the ghettoization of women's (and black, and gay) writing, the fact that men have to learn that they can read writing by women, something they often resist, the suspicion of female idiom — I mean the idiom of *Moby Dick* preferred to that of *Wuthering Heights*, two stories which greatly resemble each other; the unexamined assumption by critics that the great American novel will be written by a man — something which seems only half likely. I'm not sure the sex of the writer makes much difference to women readers because we are trained to read work by both sexes. I know as a reader I feel closer to Hemingway, a hunting, fishing sort of person from my part of Illinois and a fellow expatriot, than to English punk woman Angela Carter, or even, say, an American woman writing about an exotic New York world of shrinks and angst far from my experience.

The situation of a writer is like being veiled in Riyadh, invisible and explicit. As individuals we forget things, fail to think of the snappy response at a dinner table, are struck dumb at times we should strike back and so on. People like to meet writers, but they are mostly disappointed meeting them. It usually turns out that the

drab mortal who gratefully accepts the glass of white wine after the
reading or who plainly longs to get back to the hotel, is less than the
passionate and clever personages on her pages. Our books are ourselves veiled, assertive and bold.

Another aside: when you begin as a writer you have to learn to
accept that many strangers are going to have an opinion of your
personal defects and hangups, and that your families — this is almost
the hardest thing for writers to get used to when they begin — will
come to know that you know things about sex or swear-words they
didn't know you knew. It is amazing but true that the families of
writers often don't read them, finding it too odd or painful. And it's
a curious feature of writer photographs, that in an article containing
a review of your book, and a photo, if both are bad, it is the photo
you are apt to mind most. There is room for feeling that a reviewer
has misunderstood your work, it is a complex work, after all, capable of many interpretations, but there is no mistaking your face.

But just as there is usually a gap between the real and the ideal
character of the writer, there is also always a gap between what the
writer means to do and how his book turns out. The gap is large.
Critics tend to forget this. Any literary work is testimony to our
failed intentions. Your book never turns out to be as good as you had
hoped, back when you were thinking it up, before you went and
spoiled it by writing it down. We know, if critics don't, that our
novel is witness to our lapses of attention, hangover, diminished
stamina, boredom, unwise enthusiasms and so on. But the reader
reads, I believe, with the implicit assumption that the writer is an
authority, worthy of standing behind the work, who somehow gives
permission to read and enjoy, perhaps by his very reliability assuag-
ing the guilt we may feel at indulging in fantasy and giving ourselves
up to stories — the reasons people are apt to say that fiction is less
worthwhile than non-fiction. If, as Simon O. Lesser puts it, in his
endearing and still illuminating *Fiction and the Unconscious*, "fiction . . . provides us with images of our emotional problems
expressed in an idiom of characters and events," we need to have
confidence in the person who provides these images, just as we need
to have confidence in our grocer.

All this is to say that the writer's character comes under a certain
scrutiny as it is revealed in all the main narrative elements of a
fiction — style, subject, plot. In a poem too, no doubt. But where do
we actually find the writer? How are we aware of his or her distinc-

tive timbre, as Willa Cather called it, in narratives other than first-person ones? Style, to begin with. Take this sentence: "I won't even compare you with something I have a sort of dim stupid sense you might be and are not — for I don't in the least know that you might be it, after all, or whether, if you were, you wouldn't cease to be that something you are that makes me write to you thus." (Henry James to William Dean Howells) We recognize this writer by his style and only eventually by his rather censorious morality masked with urbanity. "Into the dark, smoky restaurant, smelling of the rich raw foods on the buffet, slid Nicole's sky-blue suit like a segment of the weather outside." That is the exuberant Fitzgerald. The narrator in *Howards End* strikes us as being like E. M. Forster, a Cambridge don, when he writes:

> The boy, Leonard Bast, stood at the extreme verge of genti-lity. . . . He knew that he was poor, and would admit it; he could have died sooner than confess any inferiority to the rich. This may be splendid of him. But he was inferior to most rich people, there is not the least doubt of it. He was not as courteous as the average rich man, nor as intelligent, nor as healthy, nor as lovable.

Here the writer and the narrator are surely one, E. M. Forster snobbish, judgmental, and perceptive. When we respond to the art-fulness or peculiarity of a phrase, I think we always attribute it not to the narrator but directly to the writer, mentally congratulating him or complaining. Beside style, choice of subject is obviously an authorial Rorschach too — your preoccupations are formed for what-ever reason, and you are the product of your experiences, though of course you can transcend them. We all tend to repeat ourselves or be known by our obsessions.

Saul Bellow dismissed plot as "unfit," seconding Gertrude Stein's opinion that it's rather low to just read novels for what happens next — Bellow mentions *Remembrance of Things Past* and *Ulysses* as novels we don't read for the story. l think we do, in fact. I've given some thought to the role of plot in writing fiction, and think it is honorable and essential, a vital activity of the novelist that has been unfairly stigmatized, with all the negative connotations of the word "plot," "plotting" meaning treachery and manipulation. About plot, the dismissive attitude grew up perhaps because, after Freud, we tried to think about all action as stemming from character, and character in turn as stemming from accidents of nurture, all determined beforehand by the logic or illogic of psychology, so that therefore "plot" with its adventitious surprises came to be seen as a mean property of the lower orders of popular literature, manipulative, not serious, and not art. By plot I mean the telling way a writer rearranges the elements of his or her experience and observation into a meaningful and absorbing ideal form that concentrates life in a way that meandering reality cannot. Bellow meant "narcotic or brainwashing entertainments, at worst breeding strange vices," which seems a little severe.

Anyone who has written a novel knows that the writer spends quite a bit of time plotting — deciding, say, whether Jeffrey will go to Detroit before or after meeting Nora, a decision with massive implications when it comes to who knows what is in the bank vault, matters wrestled with by the artist which boil down on the page to writing the one word, Thursday, instead of Sunday, and reversing two chapters — in other words in reflecting upon and manipulating a dynamic that is never expressed in words on the page, exactly, but which generates in the reader's understanding, like the synapse of a sparkplug across the empty space between the points, all the energy of the narrative. Plotting, and, more peculiarly, errors in plotting (too obvious coincidence or banal ending) are one of the invisible aspects of narration for which the writer takes responsibility and gets blamed or gets the credit. It is in his plot arrangement that the novelist is most herself, himself, where his attitudes toward life and chance, his optimism, pessimism, his merriness or mysticism speak most directly to the reader. With plot, style, subject, an author communicates the preoccupations and habits of her mind. But style, plot, and authority are the very elements that fiction has somehow been losing.

Sometimes the writer fails to communicate. To illustrate communication let's say I, the reader, am an animal lover, fond of cats and dogs. In *Wuthering Heights*, a character drowns some puppies; this may anger me with him, but I also know that Bronte is using this example of brutality to tell us something about his spiritual state. I infer that she knows how this scene will affect me because she and I are operating in the same universe of dog lovers, and thus I can have some confidence in the symbolic meanings that underlie other things that will happen in the novel.

But sometimes we don't know what a writer means. In Christina Stead's autobiographical *I'm Dying Laughing* there is a scene where the heroine and person we judge to be nearest to the writer, is debating the course of her life. This is the scene where the title line is uttered. "I'm dying laughing," so we know it is an important, portentous moment of political and artistic truth. In the course of it, Emily finds a stray cat in her Hollywood kitchen. "The kitchen was in order and faultlessly clean; but an unwashed baking dish had been put on the floor for the cat to lick at. Emily shouted, with an ugly expression, 'Who did that?'"

"She took the cat by the scruff of the neck and hauled it to the door. It was a bluish, short-haired animal with a white hourglass on the belly. It had just had kittens. It was almost starved to death. She threw it out on the hillside which rose behind the house." This passage tells us something about Emily — but what? And is it what Stead intends? We animal lovers might think Emily must be a cruel, selfish person and that Stead means us to think so, but here too are honorific images of cleanliness and aprons. One fears that Stead agrees with Emily that stray cats are a nuisance, but we are not sure. I'm afraid I think of Christina Stead as cruel to cats.

Usually, the writer, careful not to be mistaken for one of his immoral, or criminal, or foolish creations, will insert sly reservations to indicate his own disapproval of someone who mistreats cats. Parenthetically it is worth mentioning that an author will usually be confounded with his creations, and this is especially true for women writers, who are freely assumed to have the morals or tragic lives of their heroines. It is not at all unusual to receive commiserating letters, or else reproaches. How brave of you to put up with living in that slum. How sad that you lost your mother in that theater fire. I think women are unconsciously assumed to have deficient powers of invention — so what you write must be true. Paradoxically women have also always been thought, by men at least, to be great liars.

But the point is, there's a reader-writer dialogue, and if you are the writer, the reader is interested in you. We might finally ask, what are the qualities readers hope to find in you, do find in the greatest writers over the heads of their creations? What do they want from a writer? Obviously it is not personal goodness, since we tend to like writers *in propria persona* to be a little bad, like Byron, or ill-fated in some way, flawed, drunk like Hammett or Malcolm Lowry — we want them to be a little like ourselves. But not too much. Of course, just as our face is not entirely within our control, the authorial self we reveal in our books is not entirely within our control, is so much oneself that there isn't much one can do about him or her except by trying to be better or taking Prozac or undergoing religious conversion — there are only a few ways people do change. The reader can see things in us we cannot see ourselves. It's not as simple as looking to the writer for moral guidance, even though he punishes the wicked and rewards the good, or, according to the conventional ironies of our own day, punishes the good and rewards the wicked. What we want is more a sense of observantness and ambivalence, a person of two minds about the impulses of the human heart, questioning of the criteria of conventional morality. Ambivalence — the side of Shakespeare that admired Macbeth's ambition and overreaching, the thing that produced Mozart's fondness for Don Giovanni. If it is true that the greatest fiction is pervaded by a sense of the opposite (it is only inferior fiction that tends to state things too boldly in black and white, as Bellow complained), this sense is likely to issue from the writer's simultaneous grasp, as Fitzgerald put it, of two contradictory ideas. Grasp is not a bad word. We want the sense that the writer has grasped things in all their complexity and has found for them a design whose formal properties and very words release and stir us. The author can't necessarily be "good," as in faithful, sober, generous, moral in conventional terms or saintly around the house; but what he must be is a complex receptacle of virtues all the same, if forgiving and understanding are virtues. He must know something beyond himself. It's this we tend to miss in recent fiction, I think.

I've been living in France. Sometimes it's good to be away because when you re-enter you have a day or two of revealing culture shock before everything begins to seem normal to you — will be struck by how fat Americans are, how all the formerly vigorous TV journalists now seem to be wearing weird toupees, and how the serious fiction now is terse, grisly and self-pitying at the same time, mostly concerning abuse of the author's self or the indignities endured by his/her grandparents. Really, since we are here, most of our grandparents are by definition fortunate. Don't we have something else to talk about? Conceptions of virtue, for example, or the operation of our social institutions? When you come back, you hear everyone saying that our culture is finished, is unlivable, ungovernable, getting dumber. Couldn't we talk about that? I consider myself a novelist of manners, a subgenre so distant from the mainstream that this isn't usually even understood. I guess I am a novelist of manners because I came from a small Midwestern town where one could still follow the action of society on the individual. But this is old-fashioned. The great nineteenth-century novelists had one subject, which could loosely be called "how to live." We don't have that because, hey, we can't tell anyone else how to live. Victorian writers wrote about their own experience, but did so in order to put a stitch in the great tapestry of literature which tries to present the human condition. Writers today want not just money but sympathy too. I guess I think that personal witness still has value — is finally all a writer can do — but the work of a career in writing should be to refine our skills as witness and use the personal to transcend the personal.

A friend of mine showed me the manuscript of his novel. "At last I've come to understand my mother," he said. Writing a novel may indeed help you to understand your mother. Writing a novel is certainly a way of avoiding the psychoanalyst. Not even Freud wanted to tamper with the artist's mysterious powers. Roland Barthes, who seemed to have an apt observation about everything, said the motto of the writer ought to be "mad I cannot be, sane I do not deign to be, neurotic I may be," neurosis perhaps too severe a name for a powerful impulse to rearrange a less than ideal world into a better form, if only by revealing its flaws. But is American literature to become the sum of autobiographies vying for attention, like siblings on a stage? Maybe it is part of our collective loss of confidence in ourselves, an American as well as a writerly problem, that we have no larger subjects at the moment, but I think we have come to believe we have no stories to tell except, diffidently or defiantly, our own stories. And I think those are no longer enough, because we have arrived at a point in America where we can no longer understand each others' stories, or don't want to, are too ravished by the vibrancy of our own suffering, enamored of our too-facile way of appealing in all our frailty to the sympathy of others. Pain is the fashionable word. One trouble is that voices in pain tend to sound all alike, loud cries of pain drowning out thought and language. Do we have a duty to something larger? Duty is a word we tend to avoid; I know people always deplore the times they live in, but the lack of impulse to think about the inner life of others says something bad about us, and I think it is also significant, and bad, that in America, just now, no writer is considered dangerous to the state.

ALICE ADAMS

COMPLICITIES

The young girl, Nan, who has come to stay with the Travises, Jay and Mary, on their farm in southern New Hampshire—Nan is so thin that when she goes swimming in the pond deep indentations show between her small ribs. Her finely downed cheeks are hollow, her eyes the enormous eyes of a famine victim, or perhaps a sufferer from some lengthy and wasting disease. It is for this, from a desire to "build her up," to put some flesh on those bones, that her parents have sent her to the Travises for the summer. Also, there is an unspoken wish to do good to Mary and Jay, who are known to be "up against it," as the phrase went.

This was all sometime back, before any talk of eating disorders, and Nan's parents, a kindly small-town druggist and his wife, in western Pennsylvania, distant cousins of Mary Travis, do not think in terms of neurosis, rejections of love—although it does seem to them that Nan eats a fair amount, and is still morbidly thin.

Nan, at thirteen, is a fairly silly, unnaturally devious and potentially bright girl (highest I.Q. in the local eighth grade). She thinks she looks wonderful; she feels herself possessed of vast and thrilling secrets. How powerful she is! and how private; no one knows anything about her, really, not even her lover. She does not use that word in thinking about Dr. Thurston, the minister whose babysitter she occasionally is; the man who is out of his mind, deranged with love for her, she says, and certainly he acts that way, following her everywhere in his car, just to look at her as she walks home from school with friends, meeting her in that same car for rendezvous on the edge of town. Removing her clothes to cover her body with his mouth, kissing everywhere, breathing as though he might die.

Dr. Thurston (impossible to think of him as Bill, the name his fat wife uses) is one of Nan's secrets; the other is what she thinks of as "losing food," something she does in the bathroom with her fingers, after meals. Fingers down her throat, which if she has waited too long do not feel good. But it works, she can eat all she wants to and still have nothing on her bones but skin. Nothing to pinch, any-where. "I adore your pale thin body," says Dr. Thurston. "I would never profane it."

Jay Travis is a failed painter; it is hard otherwise to make a sum of his life. Once a successful advertising man, he left his wife and married his assistant, Mary, and retired to the country to paint in a serious way, as he had always intended. Periodically he takes slides and sometimes canvases down to New York, but nothing has ever panned out, and they live mostly on the foolish articles that Mary writes (she knows they are foolish) for various "ladies' magazines." For editors who are old friends, from Mary's own single New York days.

Acerbic, melancholy, and exceptionally smart, Jay often feels that he may have been better off in a commercial venture at which he could constantly scoff; he fears that he is not doing well with this serious dedication to his talents — "such as they are," as he himself would be the first to add. And this has been an especially bad year for Jay, prostate surgery in January ("Some New Year's present for a tired old cock" was his terrible joke) left him weak and further depressed. Nothing sold, and the long wet spring wore on, and now they have this skinny nymphet in the house, watching everything as fixedly as a cat.

What he truly loves, though, what Jay Travis literally adores is this farm, this lovely hillside acre with its meadows and pond, its stands of birches and hemlocks and Norway pines, its surrounding low stone fence. And the falling-down red barn, with its population of busy, half-tame cats, its bats and a family of owls. And he loves the house, low-lying, weathered to silver, its long rooms smelling of apples and of lavender. On a cane, which is half affectation, Jay paces his house and his land; he inspects the fences (for what? he wonders, whatever could happen to a very old small stone fence?) He takes dishes of milk and tuna out to the barn for the cats, and he squats there, hoping and watching for some feline form of affection, or even notice.

He watches almost translucent Nan, as she walks gingerly across the tender meadow grass and down to the pond, in her childish skimpy bathing suit — as, removing the towel from her shoulders, she shivers in the summer morning air. Occasionally Jay goes into his studio, unveils the canvas and stares at it for a while.

Always, from his window, he is hoping for a sight of Mary, whom he loves truly more than his land or his house, or his cats, or anything in life that he can imagine.

*

Mary Travis, in early middle age (she is Jay's third wife; as she herself puts it, some men just never learn) is plump and beautiful and kind and very restless. She doesn't move about a lot, as Jay always does, but she sits and stares at books and windows, occasionally getting up to polish something. She has found some wonderful lavender-smelling wax.

Or to cook. Mary likes to cook. What she serves up is in fact exceptional, great culinary triumphs, often. Even just for Jay, and recently for Jay and Nan, she makes lovely foam-light soufflés, beautiful fresh vegetable terrines, and mysterious rich soups. And magnificent cakes; she is perhaps at her best with cakes.

Having been told by Nan's parents, her cousins, of their worry over their daughter's weight, Mary watches Nan's breakfast consumption of blueberry muffins, her noontime intake of meat and cheese and fruit, her adult-sized dinners. Pleased and flattered by this new consumer, Mary feels her own views of her cooking confirmed (this is her not-so-secret vanity). But then, further observing Nan, and with greater attention, she sees no change whatsoever in the almost transparent flesh stretched over those delicate ribs. And she notes too the alacrity with which Nan heads for the bathroom after each meal, a compulsion at first excused by murmurs about her dentist: "He's an absolute maniac about post-meal brushing."

Observant and wise, Mary thinks, Can that silly little bitch be making herself throw up? How entirely disgusting, not to mention the waste.

Though poor, the Travises are fond of giving parties, on Saturdays, generally. Around six in the evening people start to arrive, in their shabby cars, seemingly from everywhere, bearing casseroles or bags of fruit, boxes of cookies. Or bottles: these parties involve an enormous number of bottles, Nan has observed. As she plans to say to her mother, they all drink like fish. An abstemious ghost, Nan hovers at the edges of these parties; she is often in white, as though to emphasize her difference.

They eat and they drink and they dance, these middle-aged hedonists.

They dance close together, mostly to old slow scratched records, old songs that Nan has barely heard of. Squinched down in an ancient leather chair with a heavy book, in a barely lit corner of the living room, Nan, who is not really reading, looks up from time to time at whatever is going on — which is not much, usually.

Until the night that Mary sings.

More absorbed than usual in her reading (it is *Gone With the Wind*), Nan has come to what she thinks of as the good parts, Rhett kissing Scarlett. She looks up with surprise at the sound of the piano, which no one ever plays; someone is playing a song she knows, "Honeysuckle Rose," a favorite of her father's.

And then suddenly Mary is standing right there by the piano. And Mary is singing.

"Don't — need — sugar —
You just have to touch my cup — "

She is singing and laughing, embarrassed, but still her voice is rich and confident and sexy — oh, so sexy! Mary is wearing a new blue dress, or maybe it's old. It is tight, some shiny material, stretched tight over those big breasts and hips. Nan, watching and listening (" — it's so sweet when you stir it up — ") experiences an extreme and nameless, incomprehensible disturbance. She feels like throwing up, or screaming, or maybe just grabbing up her knees so that her body is a tight knit ball — and crying, crying there in her corner, in the semi-dark. Is this falling in love? has she fallen in love with Mary? She thinks it is more that she wants to *be* Mary. She wants to be out there in the light, with everyone laughing and clapping. She wants to be singing, and *fat*. Oh, how wildly, suddenly, she yearns for flesh, her own flesh. Oh, fat!

"Were your other two wives as beautiful as Mary?"

None of your fucking business, is what Jay feels would have been the proper answer to this question. But Nan is only a child, he reminds himself. Also, she is their paying houseguest. And so he contents himself with saying, as vaguely as possible, "No, not exactly."

They are walking very slowly around the edge of the pond, in an

August twilight, Jay with his cane and Nan in her tiny white shorts, a skin-tight t-shirt. He had not realized before that she had breasts — or does she? Those small protuberances look a little unreal, as though she had stuffed something into a tiny bra — and it comes to Jay, with the sureness of a vision, that she must have done exactly that; she stuffed her bra, but why? why on earth? and why has she come out after him like this, interrupting his solitary stroll?

"Thin or fat?" this terrible child persists. "Your wives."

"Uh. On the plump side. I've always liked a little flesh."

But with great eagerness she has interrupted. "There's this man at home, you know? I babysit for him and his wife. He's a minister, can you believe it? And he is absolutely crazy about how thin I am. Just crazy! He follows me."

"Nan, you must avoid this man. Tell him to go away. Tell your father."

"Oh, I will. The very idea of him right now makes me — makes me want to throw up." Nan laughs immoderately at this disgusting remark.

*

"It's quite a puzzle," says Jay to Mary at dinner one night, about three weeks after that walk, that conversation with Nan. It is in fact the next-to-last night of Nan's visit, but she has gone to bed early, leaving Mary and Jay to finish what has been a celebratory feast: they are not so much celebrating her imminent departure (not explicitly, that is) but rather the fact that after years of professional drought, Jay's agent has sold a large painting, a landscape (in fact Jay's own landscape, the meadow and stand of trees next to his studio). Not only was the painting sold, there is also a commission for four more large landscapes. And that was their conversation at dinner: without Nan present, Jay was able to speak joyously of his good fortune, plans, and eagerness for work.

In terms of festivity, feasting, Mary quite outdid herself, with an oyster soufflé, and something that she calls her twenty-vegetable lamb stew, and an orange salad and a chocolate mousse. Nan, protesting fatigue, went off to bed before the mousse was served ("I may come down for a little later on, will you save some for me, Mary?") — and it is this recent shift in Nan's eating habits that they now discuss, and that Jay has just described as a puzzle.

He continues, "I'd swear she's eating less now, and at the same time she's putting on some weight."

This has been expressed more or less as a question to Mary, which Mary accepts, but she only says, "I think I understand," and she smiles.

And then, simultaneously, they lose all interest in Nan; they turn to each other as though they had been separated for some time. They look at each other with a sort of pleased surprise — and then, because it strikes them funny, they begin to laugh.

"Shall we dance?" Jay is still laughing as she says this, but that is what they do; they put on some old Glenn Miller records, from their own era, and Jimmy Lunceford and Tommy Dorsey — and they dance. Laughing and dancing, very happy with each other, they end up necking on the sofa, exhaustedly, like kids.

And that is how Nan finds them, asleep on the sofa. Mary is snoring lightly, as Jay, asleep, breathes heavily into her breast.

Giving them first a quick, disgusted look, Nan goes over to the cluttered table, which it does not occur to her to clear. There is a large, dissolving plate of chocolate mousse, all of which she spoons slowly into her mouth — ah, delicious! She will have to get the recipe for her mother, Nan thinks; they could have it at least once a week, which should mean two or three pounds right there.

Slipping back into bed without even brushing her teeth, Nan continues with what has been a waking dream, a plan: next summer, when she is sleek and fat, as fat as Mary is! she will come back up here, and Jay will fall madly in love with her. He will follow her everywhere, the way Dr. Thurston used to do. But she will say No, no kissing, even. You belong to Mary. And Mary, finding out what Nan has done, will say what a wonderful girl Nan is, how truly good, as well as beautiful, and fat.

And then Nan will leave, probably off with some boyfriend of her own by then, and Mary and Jay will mourn for her. Always. "If only Nan were with us again this summer," they will say, for years and years.

EMILY HIESTAND

SOUVENIRS ENTOMOLOGIQUES

for Jean Henri Fabre
"The Virgil of insect life he was and the Homer too."

Incomparable observer, the close-seen picture burgeons:
Behold—a dovetail moth come culling the nerves
of a local field, seeking souvenirs in red and yellow flowers:

in scarlet pompons of bee-balm, in sow-thistle,
and flanneled mullein leaves, in the common evening
primrose of roadside and flaxen waste places.

Of her mothy response to blooms, we know better
than to say *she admires them.* Yet she favors them (whisper)
above all others, settling to brush herself in lurid color.

And this: when sudden ripe with eggs, her taste for carnival fades.
She flies now in search of bedstraw green—
no other leaf, no other green for her wings of confinement.

Agreed then: of dovetail mothers we will not say *she plays*—
(save as light plays in a net over a wave playing over a shore
where hours play in declension over a fully inflected earth).

BUGS

Peconic Bay, Long Island

The ten o'clock train whistle blows
through a field of singing cicadas.
In amorous grasses, thorny rugosas
and pines, these least of creatures
wait for night to court in knock-kneed,
spindle-legged splendour, wings drawn,
in incidental pastoral, like rosin over bows:
quave   quave   breve   quave   quave

We could say the cicadas are women,
a clicking and hidden population
knitting pines and oaks to the night.
That would make the whistle male,
his lonesome song a slave to wayward ways.
But among the bugs are male and female;
male and female are among the bugs,
his ectoderm plenty exotic for her.

And the whistle calls to all, signaling
freighted commuters, ducks, and the russets
this region pulls from silt-plump fields.
Love's own keen eyes see the polished rails
crossing the fertile and syncopated field.
And each of us, dear, has ears to hear
whistle and wings antiphonal sing
treebound   traveling   treebound   traveling —
those old bugs

LAURA KASISCHKE

DRINK ME

There's blue juice and usually
someone who'll squeeze it for me from

coma and plums and the fire I set
in a circle around
my own house
to keep the other fires out. It

says DRINK ME on the bottle, and when I do
I shrink and shrink, until
I could step so easily through

the TV glass, until
my body could be carried without trouble
on the backs
of two green bees, who

bump the invisible windows, or
zig-zag all day droning
over the rotten apples, the sugar cubes, the marigolds with their
little fusty faces of grief. The air

smells ruined, bruised, fermented, sweet
as an orchard trampled
by God's big feet — while

the poison moons of Jupiter begin
to slowly drag

the milkweed up and out
of its deep, creamed, sticky sleep. Even

the goats who drink
the juice of this fruit grow
giddy and open-hearted, struggle

up to walk
on two feet
as human beings — until

they grow too fat

or tired, get mean, and gnash
at one another
with cold pink teeth. *Dear*

Mom I write home fondly
on the back of a postcard
of a frozen ocean *I*
thought I was done for a while forever

with the drinking, the drugs
and the men in leather. She

writes back *We*
know exactly what you mean — usually
it's summer here in heaven
and the goats dance stiffly

all night with the girls, and though
the ballroom smells like roses, we
always know

a tiny corpse rots under the floor.

SARAH CHAYES

THE TRIAL OF PAUL TOUVIER
An Eyewitness Account

It was a little after midnight; the chamber was almost vacant. A few black-robed lawyers spoke quietly in the aisles; a few journalists circulated in the press stand above and behind them. Then the buzzer sounded. A door opened in the back of the bulletproof box, and sharpshooters from the crack RAID police unit led Paul Touvier to his seat. He stayed half-standing, his body bent avidly toward the bench, as the judges and jurors filed in and took their seats.

The voice of Presiding Judge Henri Boulard almost broke with emotion as he began to read the verdict. To the name of each of seven men — all named but the seventh, the one who stood up to sing the air of the condemned prisoner from *Tosca* during the long night before the execution, and who is, to this day, "unknown" — the answer was "yes," he was the victim of premeditated murder. Yes, those murders "fell into the framework of a concerted plan carried out by a state practicing a policy of ideological hegemony." Yes, Paul Touvier had been an accomplice.

Silence gripped the courtroom for a moment. Then the journalists jumped to their feet and ran for the phones, and the air suddenly filled with the buzz of comments and reactions. Touvier remained utterly motionless in his bulletproof box, which alone in the stark courtroom signaled the extraordinary event that had just taken place. France had tried and condemned a Frenchman for crimes against humanity.

*   *   *

On the morning of June 29, 1944, seven men — all Jews — were lined up against the wall of a village cemetery by members of the

Lyon Militia, and shot. They were left as they lay, their names on little cards strung around their necks.

This is the act for which Touvier, Chief of Intelligence for the Lyon militia, was judged. In contrast to most criminal trials, however, the issue was not whether he had committed the act or not — there was never any doubt Touvier had organized the shooting — but whether that act amounted to a crime against humanity, and thus merited trial and punishment fifty years later.

Touvier's defense attorney did everything in his power to keep the proceedings focused on the single incident of June 29. But because of the nature of the trial, the moral and political context was unveiled, fitfully, over the days of testimony by eyewitnesses and experts. The context is Vichy, France's wartime government. "Vichy," said the Public Prosecutor, Hubert de Touzalin, pleading for the State against Touvier, "enacted its first piece of anti-Jewish legislation on October 3, 1940. The Germans weren't even there yet to ask that it be done." He paused. His bony head, emerging from his crimson

Lawyers for the civil parties to the suit in the trial of Paul Touvier, March 1994. Courtesy *Le Progrès*

robes like some prehistoric bird's, turned to the jurors. "I didn't realize this myself until a few days ago."

It is this combination of fascination and startled ignorance about Vichy that gave the trial of Paul Touvier its significance. The years between 1940 and 1944 keep returning to haunt France, with the regularity of a nightmare a sleeper tries to suppress. A number of books have appeared in the last year, investigating various aspects of "the past that won't pass."[1] The character of the Vichy government and the behavior of the men who outlived it have become matters of intense public debate. Even President Mitterrand, after a book by journalist Pierre Péan about his World War II activities sparked a national uproar, was impelled to grant an extraordinary hour-long television interview on the subject. "France has never so criticized Vichy as in the past few years," he remarked.

This newfound curiosity is the inevitable consequence of a decades-long exercise in denial initiated by none other than Charles de Gaulle: "The Republic never ceased to exist. . . . Vichy was, and remains, null and void," he said to one of the leaders of the internal Resistance in August of 1944.[2] The restored French Republic did conduct an *Epuration* after the war: a wave of trials of suspected collaborators throughout the country, which lasted from 1944 to 1951. Some 80,000 people were condemned to penalties ranging from execution to "national indignity." (Seventy-three thousand were acquitted.) Still, when asked today, former Resistants on the right as well as the left say that the process was cut short, and that while certain categories paid heavily, others, such as functionaries and entrepreneurs, did not. In the name of national reconciliation, de Gaulle aborted the effort to identify and punish those who had joined in Vichy's gamble on the "New Europe." And as a balm to the national pride, he originated the legend, taught to generations of schoolchildren afterward, of a widespread French Resistance.

President Georges Pompidou followed de Gaulle's lead in urging silence. "Are we to keep eternally bloody the wounds of our national discord?" he wondered aloud during an extraordinary press conference he gave in 1972, after his decision to pardon Paul Touvier. "Has not the time come to drop a veil, to forget the days when the French disliked one another, tore one another apart, even killed one another?"[3]

François Mitterrand, for his part, never made a secret of his preference for letting sleeping dogs lie. As the Touvier trial drew to its close, a 1992 interview was reprinted in a provincial newspaper, and flew from hand to hand in the press stand. "You know, there were lots of trials after the war," Mitterrand had said. "It's difficult to rejudge things half a century later. . . . These are old men now. Putting them on trial doesn't make much sense any more." Closing arguments by lawyers for the civil parties to the suit — including by Mitterrand's former Minister of Foreign Affairs, Roland Dumas — took time out to castigate the President's attitude.

Mitterrand's answers to the TV anchorman's delicately-posed questions in September were hardly designed to calm the newly-raw emotions, either. Asked about Vichy's anti-Jewish laws, he reacted almost testily, "You say 'anti-Jewish laws.' In fact — though this excuses nothing — they were laws against foreign Jews, which I was totally unaware of. . . . As for the concentration camps, I was like any other relatively well-informed Frenchman: I didn't know much." Such a declaration, coming from a man who had worked in the Vichy government from early 1942 until mid-1943, and who maintained close contacts with the decision-makers in Marshal Pétain's immediate entourage, was hard to believe.

Mitterrand's discussion of his long-standing friendship with Vichy Police Secretary-General René Bousquet was even more disconcerting. The French police had served as the obedient and constant executor of SS orders throughout the war, and Bousquet had approved and organized most of the deportations from France, including the midsummer round-up of over 13,000 Jews in Paris in 1942 (the *Rafle du Vel d'Hiv*). He was assassinated in 1993, shortly before his *own* trial for crimes against humanity. Mitterrand defended his continued association with Bousquet by saying: "He was accused of horrific acts, but he was aquitted [in 1949] by a High Court of Justice . . . with felicitations, practically. He re-entered normal life, and he was received everywhere. . . . He was an interesting fellow, very well connected in political and financial circles."[4] Yet any Resistant — a title Mitterrand proudly bears — knew precisely what role the French police played during World War II, and did not need to wait for "new evidence" of Bousquet's responsibility, unearthed in 1986.

Mitterrand also admitted, toward the end of the interview, that as President he had intervened to delay judicial proceedings against former war criminals. "My duty is to make sure that the French become reconciled with each other after a time. I am not naturally hostile to punishment. But pardon exists also, and if it can serve French unity, I'm for it."

The notion of pardon, as well as consideration of who has the right to bestow it, was one of the principal themes during the trial of Paul Touvier.

What was perhaps more interesting than Mitterrand's responses, or even the revelations that sparked them — since they hardly did more than confirm or complete what few people could honestly claim not to have known — was the orgy of national soul-searching they set off. The Socialist Party locked itself into its headquarters for several days of anguished recrimination. The media belabored the subject with endless commentary and analysis. Péan's book coincided with the wrenching process of recognizing the profound contradictions and traces of evil within its body politic that France is finally undertaking in earnest.

Movies such as *The Sorrow and the Pity*, by Marcel Ophuls, Louis Malle's *Au Revoir les Enfants*, and more recently, Claude Chabrol's *The Eye of Vichy*, have been part of this process, as well as books. But judicial procedures, in a kind of graduated series, have played a critical role in reminding the French of their ambiguous past. The easiest case to tackle was that of Klaus Barbie, in 1989. It was no great feat, at such a late date, to gather a consensus in favor of bringing the detested and still well-remembered German Gestapo chief ("the Butcher of Lyon") to justice. Barbie ran the Gestapo's Fourth Section — charged with the suppression of Jews and "Terrorists" — in Lyon, during the last two years of the war. Apart from ordering the round-up and deportation of Jews, he effected a number of bloody operations against Resistance *maquis* in the region, and arrested Jean Moulin. He was known, incidentally, for taking pleasure in conducting interrogations himself.

Paul Touvier was another matter. He is French, and, thanks in part to the French Catholic Church, managed to hide out until the postwar fever to "purify" was replaced by a fever to forget. (News that the French secret service had offered him a job in the early 1960s, when he was still in "hiding," raised hardly a whisper during his trial.) A public trial would inevitably stir waters that de Gaulle had so abruptly calmed at the end of the war. It would also force the issue of responsibility — not only the responsibility of the Vichy government, but the responsibility of millions of French men and women who, in their reverent affection for Philippe Pétain and their fear of disorder, chose not to question the state that ruled them.

Of course, Touvier himself is a kind of aberration, an extremist during the war and an outcast afterward. In that respect he differs from a Bousquet, who enjoyed decades of postwar respectability, or a Maurice Papon, Vichy Prefect of Bordeaux, who held a number of administrative offices before becoming Prefect of the Paris police from 1958 to 1966. Their trial would have had an entirely different significance. Nevertheless, bringing Touvier to justice was a genuine step in France's slow and sometimes reluctant effort to discern the truth at last; indeed, the fact that the trial happened "fifty years later" is perhaps what gave it a special moral significance.

*   *   *

A group of historians, including Robert O. Paxton of Columbia University, were called as witnesses — unheard-of in a French court of law. Paxton's work had helped trigger the first shock-waves of France's awakening in the mid-1970s. *Vichy France* described the French government's efforts to negotiate cooperation with Germany in return for membership in the postwar "New Europe." It revealed the police's increasingly compromised role maintaining order in "free" as well as occupied territory. It demonstrated the existence of an indigenous National Revolution, influenced by German thinking, perhaps, but perfectly and profoundly French.

For five weeks, defense attorney Jacques Trémolet de Villers would use every bit of his skill to prevent this kind of information from entering the courtroom, and he was not about to spare Robert Paxton. No sooner had the professor finished his testimony than Trémolet was on his feet. "A historian," he said, "is not a witness. A witness is somebody who lived through an event, which is what gives him the right to testify under oath. A historian, by profession, relies on hearsay. What he has to say isn't testimony, it's opinion." Trémolet turned to face Paxton, still standing at the metal bar in the middle of the room. "On the jacket of your book," he said, holding it up, "the critics call your view of this period 'revolutionary.' Very good. Congratulations. That means that before you, other historians had a different theory. And others, after you, will doubtless have another." He paused. "Let's say you were a moment in the history of Vichy."

Paxton, for a moment, seemed to grow pale.

Some facts, nevertheless, are established. Vichy, in the person of its Law and Order Minister, founded the Militia late in the war as a kind of auxiliary police to hunt down Resistants, Communists, and other members of the "Anti-France," and to "fight continuously against the Jewish leprosy." It was, from its foundation, a political formation. "We have clearly manifested our desire to install an authoritarian national socialist regime in France, so that France can take her place in tomorrow's Europe," said Law and Order Minister Joseph Darnand during his address inaugurating the new organization.[5] Militiamen were to be non-Jewish volunteers, Frenchmen by birth, who were "morally ready and physically able not only to support the new State by their action, but to contribute to internal order."[6]

Details of how the Militia went about its sworn duty in Lyon filled out the context at Touvier's trial. There was the Jesuit high school that served as Headquarters, photographed from every angle. Presiding Judge Boulard leaned across the bench to hand three black-and-white glossies to a witness, who nodded, and recalled the courtyard downstairs, jammed with looted furniture. ("Not looted," Touvier interrupted, "confiscated.") There was René Zeizig's description of the Militiamen arresting his father. "He won't be needing that where he's going," they said to Zeizig's wife, shoving back the raincoat she held out to him. The next day they returned with a truck and emptied Zeizig's general store. There was Edouard Lew, in tears at the bar as he told how the Militiamen burst into the restaurant where he was eating dinner with his young friend Claude Benzimra. Benzimra had gotten false papers that very day, but Lew didn't know what name they were in. So, though he convinced the Militiamen to leave him off at the train station, he couldn't cover his friend, who died the next day at Rillieux. The anguish in Lew's voice testified to his unquenchable remorse. There were allusions to Marguerite Flavien, a captured Resistant, who jumped out the second floor window rather than be interrogated by Touvier's men.

*   *   *

What complicated the analysis of this context was the way French jurisprudence has dealt with the question of crimes against humanity — the issue at the very core of the trial.

"The definition of crimes against humanity—in its current version—can be summarized in one sentence, which is ten lines long, contains fourteen verbs, of which one is the active participle." Hubert de Touzalin, with his bony head, his blood-red robes tipped in ermine, and his rigidly-organized oral argument, began his treatment of the subject with this caution. "Jurists," he added, "are not by nature prone to simplify."

It was in 1964 that France first incorporated crimes against humanity into its criminal code. The law refers directly to the wording of the charter establishing the international military tribunal at Nuremberg. A crime against humanity, according to the formula, consists in any barbarous act—assassination, deportation, enslavement, extermination—committed against civilian populations, during or after the war.

Over the twenty-one years it took to bring the Touvier case to trial, the courts revisited the definition at least half a dozen times. In 1985, in the course of proceedings against Klaus Barbie, the High Court referred to crimes against humanity as inhuman acts, committed in a systematic fashion "in the name of a state carrying out a policy of ideological hegemony." The phrase would come back to haunt every subsequent judicial or popular treatment of the issue.

The most spectacular opinion was the one handed down by the Paris Chambre d'Accusation on April 13, 1992—dismissing all charges against Paul Touvier. After 199 pages of discussion, the Court turned to the question of whether Vichy "was or was not a *State practicing a policy of ideological hegemony.*" What followed was an extraordinary reading of history. While, according to the court, "a certain 'ideology' may indeed have been present within the Vichy regime," it was really only a "constellation of 'good intentions' and political animosities." "One can discern a nostalgia for tradition, for the rural and artisanal world of yester-year, an attachment to Christianity, a propensity toward contrition in the face of the difficulties of the day," but "at no time did the Vichy regime have either the aim or the opportunity of establishing any kind of domination, or imposing a conquering ideology." The collaboration with Germany was "at its root, a pragmatic policy."

What the court passed over unmentioned were some of the defining characteristics of the Vichy State: the Jewish Code, which barred "Israelites" from public office, from teaching, or playing in the same playgrounds as their Christian compatriots; the posters in every village square explaining how to pick out a Jewish profile; the deportations organized and carried out by the French police; the concentration camps in Drancy or Pithiviers, where Jews, Communists, and other suspected dissidents were interned before being deported; the "Mandatory Labor Service," for which thousands of young men were rounded up and sent in closed boxcars to German factories; or the material support for the Nazi war effort, which was, according to an official report, the largest in Europe. "No other country contributes nearly as high a total for German armaments and even goods imports."[7]

"In consequence," the court wrote, "the Vichy state, whatever may have been its weaknesses, its cowardices, and its ignominies, cannot be considered to have belonged to the category of . . . states practicing a policy of ideological hegemony." In other words, while Germans or Italians could be guilty of crimes against humanity, a Frenchman, by definition, could not.

It was not until November 27, 1992, that the Public Prosecutor and the civil parties to the suit won their first decisive victory. The High Court invalidated the decision in Touvier's favor, for one out of the six counts, in a ruling that invited further analysis of the Vichy regime. For, said the judges, nothing in the texts rules that only a perfectly totalitarian regime could have practiced the famous "policy of ideological hegemony." Vichy itself, as fractured as it was, might have done so.

Nearly a year later, a second Chambre d'Accusation, in Versailles, indicted Paul Touvier for complicity with crimes against humanity. The judges' reasoning, however, was much more limited than that of their predecessors. "It is important to emphasize," they wrote, "that according to the terms of the Statute of the International Military Tribunal of Nuremberg . . . only the policy of a European Axis country can be incriminated" for crimes against humanity. Vichy, in other words, could not be so accused.

Touvier's guilt or innocence would thus depend entirely on whether links of complicity could be established between him and the occupying power. His responsibility "is engaged solely by virtue of his personal actions," the court continued, finding it "unnecessary" to "follow the civil parties' argument that the Militia and the government of the French state . . . were themselves accomplices to the Nazi state in its policy of ideological hegemony."

Thus, according to this ruling, if Paul Touvier organized the shooting at Rillieux under German orders, then he committed a crime against humanity. But if he acted on his own initiative — or in service to France's indigenous National Revolution — then he was "merely" guilty of a war crime, for which the statute of limitations ran out twenty-seven years ago.

*   *   *

This irony provoked various logical contortions, notably on the part of the lawyers for the civil parties to the suit. (There were about thirty of them: a bevy of black robes occupying the entire left side of the chamber.) For, where the argument for years has been that Touvier acted alone — as a way of fixing responsibility on Touvier himself and countering any notion of external duress — suddenly the same lawyers were insisting on a direct Gestapo order — to stay within the strict legal definition of complicity.

It was the venerable Joë Nordmann who led the about-face. Nordmann's mere presence at the trial was one of its most dramatic elements. As a Communist and a Jew, disbarred and forced to live in hiding during World War II, he symbolized everything Touvier had sworn to destroy, and his eighty-four years cried out a vigorous defiance to the idea that Touvier was too old to be judged. "We were wrong," Nordmann summed up, unashamed, in his closing statement. The trial, he said, "taught us things we didn't know before" — in spite of twenty-one years combing through the record. New evidence, it seemed, proved that the Germans might have ordered the execution of the seven Jews after all, for the Nazis did care enough about the assassination of a loyal Vichy minister, even in 1944, to demand retribution.[8]

At the Brasserie du Palais across the street from the courthouse, where lawyers and journalists shared a table during the recesses, the attorneys commented on their collective about-face with a shrug of the shoulders. What mattered was convicting Touvier. Not all of them fell into line, of course. Young Arno Klarsfeld — son of the famed Nazi-hunters Serge and Béate Klarsfeld — with his shoulder-length hair and swashbuckling cowboy boots under his lawyer's robes, made a point of provoking his colleagues (whom he referred to as "vulgar old fish" in an interview published during the trial). In the courtroom his every question turned into an involved monologue, which the judge had to forcibly interrupt. Klarsfeld's point, however, was worth taking: it's the jurisprudence, he argued, that's twisted, and the jury needn't swallow its reasoning. They could convict Touvier without accepting the thesis of a direct German order. "For if you do," Klarsfeld said, "you don't just make the Militia the Gestapo's hatchet man, you also allow for the idea that it was a shield, protecting the French from Nazi excesses."

*   *   *

Not only do lawyers on the same team disagree in open court, but under French procedure, the presiding judge conducts all the questioning, and thus profoundly affects the atmosphere. Judge Henri Boulard, in this case, seemed never to have encountered a non-leading question. For instance: "You hired some pretty unsavory characters for your Militia, didn't you, Touvier?" (Answer: "Nobody ever used altar boys for police work.") Or: "Well, you were the Chief, weren't you? You were responsible for what went on, weren't you? Hein? Hein?"

Touvier has a faint voice, like a candle about to go out. At the slightest interruption, he would stop: "I can't remember." "I'm too tired, I can't go on." This was his ploy, and to make him speak, one would have had to apply a kind of determined patience, almost coax him. But no one in the room, least of all the judge, was willing to do so.

Boulard's patent discomfort, expressed by his awkward, almost adolescent gestures and his petulant rebukes, was a heightened reflection, indeed a caricature, of the reigning atmosphere. It was as though everybody, lawyers and judges alike, was concerned above all with proving their own political virtue, their own innocence of France's crimes. The journalists' tribune and the cameras recording the proceedings for posterity proved irresistible, and questions ostensibly directed at Touvier were clearly posed for the benefit of that audience. Consequently, though the trial succeeded in judging Touvier, it largely failed in its second objective: obliging him — after two condemnations in absentia, after his prolonged siege of President Pompidou to obtain amnesty, after forty-nine years in hiding — to explain himself.

*   *   *

In spite of these flaws, and in spite of Touvier's efforts to guard his tongue, a clearer picture of him emerged as the trial progressed. When the guards first led him haltingly to his seat, a hush fell in the crowded chamber, as all of us stared at him, unabashedly, comparing his features to the blurry photographs that were all most of us had ever seen. Touvier sat unflinching under the weight of our gaze, like a wax statue in his glass box. Gradually, we grew used to his presence, and began to turn our eyes elsewhere, but his eerie stillness, his wax-like immobility, came to represent him in our imaginations.

Every time Touvier spoke—which always came as something of a surprise—he unmasked himself. "I believe in God all-powerful, creator of heaven and earth, and in His only son . . ." he recited, when asked to explain his religious convictions. "You see?" he added, "Not a jot of anti-Semitism in it."

And the "Jewish leprosy" he had sworn to combat? Or the song about "Israel, ignoble putrefaction" that he and the other Militiamen sang? "I didn't see anything anti-Semitic in all that," Touvier answered. "It was just words, no malicious intent."

His testimony was laced with similar enormities. Like others, he professed an ignorance of events taking place in the France he was supposedly fighting for that would have been incredible in a Breton peasant, let alone the chief intelligence officer in one of Vichy France's most important cities. The promulgation of the Jewish codes had "escaped him," as had the deportations.

"Mr. Touvier," said Judge Marie-Thérèse Lesueur de Givry, who asked one or two crisp, *non*-leading questions per session. "You told us yesterday that you didn't know Jews had to wear yellow stars, or that their identity cards had to be stamped with the word 'Israelite.' Could you tell me: did you, as chief of intelligence for the Lyon Militia, ever check a Jew's identity?"

"I don't remember," said Touvier.

The lapses of memory were impossible to take at face value, even in an old man under medication for cancer and depression. They were too common and too convenient—and especially when another side of him slipped out:

"When Lyon was liberated, on September 4," Judge Henri Boulard began one day—

"September 3," snapped Touvier. The chamber froze.

Other responses, as outrageous or even nonsensical as the lies, were perhaps more revealing, for they were spoken innocently, without intention to deceive. It was as though Touvier still lived sealed in a wartime universe that had grown unintelligible to his audience. He was asked about his brother, for example, who had left the country in 1943 to join the Free French. "So he was your opposite," Boulard remarked. "Why opposite?" answered Touvier. "He was a patriot, too. I even went down to Marseille to see him off to North Africa."

A strange patriotism, Touvier's, that could allow him to accept the induction of his supervisor, Law and Order Minister Joseph Darnand, into the Waffen SS. At the ceremony, Darnand swore obedience to Hitler "unto death." "We didn't know the words of the oath," said Touvier, quietly. "Besides, Darnand must have had his reasons. Maintaining good relations with the Germans was indispensable for the Militia to continue its action. Darnand was always with the Marshal; the Marshal was always behind him, so it was alright."

Answers like this, in their total incongruity, offered a sudden glimpse back into the France where Vichy could have happened: the France that accorded Marshal Pétain an all-embracing reverence that rejected closer scrutiny, the France that was at least as afraid of disorder and its own Left as it was of Hitler.

This strange sense that the court was in the presence of some kind of specimen, perfectly preserved from the effects of time by the hermetic existence he had led since 1945, was increased by a surprise exhibit. A stack of cardboard boxes, piled on a table just in front of the judges' bench, had gone unnoticed until Boulard decided to open one, more or less at random, on the trial's seventh day. They were Touvier's effects—notebooks and various Nazi insignia—seized when he was arrested in 1989. "Oh, don't bother with that, it's nothing," Touvier said, as the judge began digging through. Boulard pulled out a notebook and began turning the pages. It was a kind of commonplace book, in which Touvier had carefully pasted newspaper clippings, underlined or annotated, or copied out poems or prayers, or noted down his reactions to television programs or the news of the day.

Boulard stopped, and began reading out loud: "March 29, 1986. There's an article on the appointment of Claude Malhuret to the Secretariat for Human Rights. The words, 'sinister Jewish merchant' are written across his picture." He turned the page: "April 26, next to a clipping on the upcoming trial of Klaus Barbie, Touvier writes:

'Same odious subject: vengeance. And Msgr. Decourtray has himself interviewed by the *Globe*—revolting Jewish magazine.' In May, Touvier refers to anchorwoman Anne Sinclair as 'Jewish offal.'"

The notebook goes on and on. On every page, anti-Semitic slogans are scribbled next to the names of French personalities. References to suspected Nazi war criminals—Mengele, Demjanjuk, Barbie—are collected with avid care, their protestations of innocence copied out and underlined by way of commentary. Philippe Pétain ("a martyr—a *real* one") is a constant presence, always deferentially referred to as "the Marshal." The book is the archive of a mind that never left the Militia.

*   *   *

"Time has been one of the main themes of this trial," said lawyer Michel Zaoui, one of the last to plead against Touvier. From where we were sitting, above and behind him, his head, with its ruff of graying hair, was like a clown's. But his argument, after four full days of often theatrical soliloquy on the part of twenty-three of his colleagues, rang with lucidity. "Time normally leads to metamorphosis," he continued. "We do not claim Touvier's notebooks prove the crime against humanity. They don't. But they reveal something important: the complete lack of change in Touvier's character. He did not take advantage of the time he had to take stock of his actions. Fifty years have passed and he is the same man. Therefore, you should judge him as though it were the morning after Rillieux."

Time, indeed, was the element that set this trial apart. "Fifty years later, it's impossible to conduct a fair trial," Trémolet de Villers roared one day, in the trial's first major incident. This had been his constant refrain, repeated every time he challenged a witness's memory or defended his client's forgetfulness. When Judge Boulard read from the 1945 deposition of one of Touvier's subordinates, saying he was "zealous against the Jews," Touvier answered back: "You can't take what people said at the end of the war at face value. They'd say anything to get off." Trémolet de Villers leapt in to support his client: "Proceedings from the Courts of Justice are not valid evidence. Those trials were hardly more than courts-martial. They were dispatched in a matter of hours, and there was a firing squad out the back door. If you could ask Gonnet or de Bourmont now, in the safety of this chamber, what they think, you might get a different answer. But you can't ask them. They're dead. Fifty years later, it's impossible to conduct a fair trial!"

"And whose fault is it?" shouted a voice from the ranks of lawyers opposite Trémolet. The feeling of outrage was palpable. "If you please!" Judge Boulard interjected. French judges do not wield a gavel.

It was Touvier, of course, who had exerted every effort to post-pone his day of reckoning. Observers during and after the trial pointed out the irony: that if he had turned himself over to the authorities in 1950, or even 1960, his sentence would have been much lighter — a year or so in jail, if that. The forty-year-long flight from justice he chose instead added a further element of symbolism to his story, for what it revealed about France's hidden complicities and inclination to look the other way.

His flight began when Touvier knocked on an abbot's door, as the advancing Allied armies pushed through Lyon in September, 1944. The instinctive appeal to the church was to recur again and again. For a day or two, or a week — it is difficult to reconstruct the chronology — he hid out with the Abbot Vautherin, then with a certain priest, Father Ancel, who was a friend of the family. It went on for three years like that, in spite of multiple arrest warrants and condemnations in absentia. Then, in July 1947, he was stopped in Paris by the French Secret Service. They held him at headquarters for five days of interrogation, after which he "escaped" — by walking down the back stairs and out the door.

Between 1949 and 1968, in spite of two death sentences, Touvier lived peacefully, if discreetly, with his wife and two children in his family home in Chambéry, east of Lyon. It is during the second half of this period that he began an obsessive campaign for pardon, which was eventually to gain the support of a number of religious, political, and cultural figures. Not until 1972, after the pardon he finally won sparked a shockwave of public opposition, did Touvier take flight again, though he was, technically, a citizen like any other. The Secret Service came to his house to let him know he was no longer safe. In 1973 the first charges for crimes against humanity were brought against him, but Touvier, officially, had disappeared. When he was finally tracked down and arrested in 1989, it was, unsurprisingly, in a monastery.[9]

*   *   *

Claude Grellier was the third of four investigating judges assigned to Touvier's case between 1973 and 1994. It was his decision to use the gendarmes rather than the national police to search for Touvier that eventually led to his arrest. Grellier is a slim, thoughtful man, who speaks with conviction, but discretion. "My task was to find out if he was still alive," he says, noting that an obituary had been published in 1984. For Grellier, the search for Touvier was "intriguing," almost like a game. "The enigma wasn't very hard to pierce," he says. "Up till then, no one had really bothered to do what it took to look for him. No unit of the police was particularly motivated."

Grellier defends the propriety of bringing Touvier to trial, even in the face of such fundamental juridical principles as the non-retroactivity of the law and the statute of limitations. "We're obviously in a domain where juridical notions have a hard time adapting," he says. "I accept that one can debate the issue of imprescriptablility or retroactivity in purely juridical — that is rational or pseudo-rational terms — but I don't find it aberrant on the level of conscience to try Touvier, to make him explain his actions to a jury of his peers."[10]

By the time the trial was held, most observers, jurists and historians alike, agreed with this view: an extraordinary crime merits extraordinary justice.

*   *   *

To Jacques Trémolet de Villers, however, such justice was no justice at all. Trémolet was omnipresent during the trial, delicately flicking back the sleeves of his robe as he reached for a document, pouncing whenever the proceedings strayed from the facts of Rillieux. Indeed, if anything kept this from being a show trial, it was his skill. His closing statement was the apogee: for five and a half hours, without a note and with only one pause, in a voice sometimes hoarse with emotion, sometimes low and almost pleading, he harangued the jurors and the judges. He deployed the entire range of his arguments, but time remained a primary theme.

"You can't erase fifty years with a stroke of the pen," he began. "You cannot ignore the depth and weight of time." Time, in Trémolet's view, not only erases evidence and clouds memories, making it difficult to discern the reality of an event, but it also precludes objective judgment about the event's significance. "At Nuremberg," he said, "a total of two people were judged exclusively for crimes against humanity. One of them, the Governor of Vienna, von Schirach, was charged with the deportation of 50,000 Jews from Vienna. He was sentenced to twenty years in jail. In 1946, for acts of that magnitude, which were an integral part of the 'concerted plan,' he got twenty years. And now, in 1994, before a French criminal court, the prosecution is demanding life imprisonment for the murder of seven Jews? What planet are we on? This is delirium!"

Trémolet could have chosen a number of examples, many of them closer to home: Bousquet's virtual acquittal after the war, for instance, or the pardon that Karl Oberg, chief of the SS in France, received at the hands of Charles de Gaulle.[11]

The simple answer to this discrepancy—as articulated by Joë Nordmann among others—is that just because some of the guilty were let off too easily or not brought to trial at all, doesn't mean Touvier should benefit from the same error.

Another opinion often voiced during the trial is that France did not immediately appreciate the full significance of what happened during World War II. "It wasn't until the '60s and '70s that there was a kind of revelation—a sudden realization that we hadn't taken account of the horror," says historian Yves-Marie Hilaire, a member of the commission appointed by the Archbishopric of Lyon to study the links between Touvier and the Church. "One must remember that most Jews sent to Auschwitz or the other extermination camps never came back. And the ones who did come back didn't speak about it for years and years. They didn't want to stand out, or they were afraid they wouldn't be believed."[12] In the approximately 120,000 postwar trials, the subject of deportation was almost never mentioned; the charges were exclusively military: treason, communication with the enemy.

The passage of time, in other words, was actually needed to arrive at a just punishment, because a true understanding of the nature of the crime could not exist in 1945. In this sense, the fact that Touvier managed to escape for so many years can almost be seen as a blessing—as though destiny had preserved him until France, endowed with a new and deeper understanding of its past, was ready. Judging him became a way of expressing the nation's new maturity. That it was Paul Touvier and not another who was reserved for this role might be considered unlucky for him, but not intrinsically unjust.

Lawyer Michel Zaoui added another dimension to this discussion, emphasizing time's capacity to calm the passions. "Fifty years were necessary to speak 'without hate and without fear,' " he said, repeating the words of the oath administered to witnesses in French courts. The first generation wanted vengence, Zaoui continued, and the second wanted to forget. "Only with the third generation can justice be rendered, with all serenity."

*   *   *

Night was falling when the court recessed to deliberate, ending the five-week-long drama. Actors and audience alike tumbled out into the darkened street, and swarmed toward the cluster of cafes by the courthouse gates, famished. Joë Nordmann, with his snow-white hair and eagle nose, stood in the glare of a television light in the middle of the street. The reporters for NPR and the BBC sat at a minuscule round table outside the Brasserie, filling in the lacunae in each others' notes. Inside, Trémolet de Villers and a huge party occupied a centrally-located table, while the brother of one victim and the son of another took up tables nearby.

Outside, on a street corner, Larry Glaeser stood waiting for his father, Henri, who was eighteen when *his* father was shot at Rillieux. Glaeser is a tall young man, with liquid blue-green eyes and a shy apology in his voice. "This trial was truly an event," he said. "From the very start, the fundamental questions were posed, and for that I'm grateful. I myself learned a lot about Vichy, even though Touvier, the Church, Vichy, are names I grew up with. And I'm grateful for another thing, too. This trial allowed me to discover my grandfather. He was a mythic figure for me, and so it was hard for me to know who he really was. Now he's a man again."

This is perhaps the real significance of France's continued, almost obsessive fascination with Vichy. The country is trying to turn the Occupation, and those who made it what it was, from a myth back into a reality that can be accepted, comprehended, and put to rest. But instead of disappearing, the livid ghost of Vichy has grown more distinct with each successive exercise in self-examination. The exorcism is not yet over.

NOTES

[1] I quote from the title of one of them: Eric Conan and Henry Rousso, *Le passé qui ne passe pas* (Paris: Fayard, 1994). See also Pierre Péan, *Une jeunesse française* (Paris: Fayard, 1994) on Mitterrand, Gérard Boulanger, *Maurice Papon* (Paris: Seuil, 1994), Pascale Froment, *René Bousquet* (Paris: Stock, 1994), René Raffin and Alain Jakubovics, *Touvier: Histoire du procès* (Paris: Julliard, 1995).

[2] Quoted in Henry Rousso, *Le Syndrome de Vichy, de 1944 à nos jours*, 2nd edition (Paris: Seuil, 1990), 31.

[3] See René Rémond, et al., *Paul Touvier et l'église* a careful study of the links between Touvier and the French church commissioned by the Archbishop of Lyon, Cardinal Decourtray (Paris: Fayard, 1992), 380.

[4] Bousquet's role in the deportation of over 70,000 Jews from France was never brought up at his 1949 trial. The court concluded that "as regrettable as Bousquet's behavior may have been, it does seem that he knowingly accomplished acts that were destructive to the national defense, and thus he should be acquited. However, in accepting the post of Secretary General of the Police, Bousquet became guilty of the crime of national indignity." His sentence to five years of national indignity (during which time a person may neither vote nor be elected to any position of social responsibility, nor inherit property) was revoked as soon as it was pronounced, however. See *Le Monde*, September 14, 1994.

[5] Quoted in J. Delerrie de Bayac, *Histoire de la Milice: 1918–1945* (Paris: Fayard, 1969), 164.

[6] Article 1 of the law establishing the Militia (Law 63, Jan. 30, 1943) in *ibid.*, 664.

[7] Richard Hemmen, chief economic delegate to the Wiesbaden Armistice Commision, quoted in Robert Paxton, *Vichy France* (New York: Columbia University Press, 1972), 144.

[8] The seven Jews, plus two other non-Jews, eventually separated from the group, were rounded up on the day and evening after the assassination of Philippe Henriot, Vichy Information Minister, whose twice-daily exhortations were the mainstay of Radio Vichy. Reprisals were also mounted in the towns of Macon, Toulouse, and Grenoble.

[9] For details on Touvier's flight and other elements of biography, see René Rémond, et al., or Laurent Greilsamer and Daniel Schneidermann, *Un certain Monsieur Paul* (Paris: Fayard, 1994).

[10] Personal interview: March 11, 1994.

[11] Not to mention the dozens of war criminals who lived peacefully in Germany under successive postwar governments. See Hannah Arendt, *Eichmann in Jerusalem* (New York: Penguin, 1965).

[12] Personal interview: March 5, 1994.

ABBE SMITH

ON REPRESENTING A VICTIM OF CRIME

Rebecca Wight and Claudia Brenner fell in love in Graduate School. In May of 1988, when Rebecca was still in school in Virginia and Claudia was living and working in upstate New York, they decided to meet for a weekend of hiking and camping. They picked a halfway spot, on the Appalachian Trail in the Michaux State Forest, in central Pennsylvania. They both loved the outdoors and were avid hikers.

They met at a prearranged outpost, parked their cars, donned their packs, and set off. They spent the day hiking, at times arm in arm, ambling leisurely, and, at times, covering serious ground. The weather was unusually warm for that time of year. The trail was serene and untrammeled; it was still early in the season.

They shared a sleeping bag and spent the first night tucked close together. The air outside the tent was clean and crisp and cool. The only sound was the night.

The next morning, after breakfast, Rebecca headed for the outhouse, which was next to a lean-to. She was naked, believing no one else was near. She and Claudia had encountered no other hikers there. She was startled to find a man, ragged and haggard, standing in the lean-to. "D'ya have any cigarettes on you?" he asked. "No," Rebecca replied, annoyed by both his presence and his question. She was naked. Of course she had no cigarettes "on" her.

She swiftly headed back to the tent to tell Claudia that there was a strange man lurking around, and they'd better pack up and go. They collected their things and departed, passing the man on their way out.

This essay is taken from a volume of eight stories about how law operates in people's everyday lives, *Law Stories*, edited by Gary Bellow and Martha Minow, to be published by the University of Michigan Press next spring.

They walked for about a mile before stopping at a crossroads to consult the map and consider their options. As they studied the map, the strange man appeared again. This time he had a rifle across his shoulders, his arms slung over each end. He mocked the women with his posture and his words. "What, are you lost already?" he sneered.

"No, we're not lost," Claudia replied, intending to end the conversation. "Are *you*?" She and Rebecca went back to their map, ignoring the man. They picked a route that would take them far off the main trail, to regain their seclusion. They wanted to be left alone.

They hiked three and a half circuitous miles into the wild, far off the well-traveled paths, far from other human contact. They found an ideal spot to set up camp, near a stream. They made camp and a cold jug of iced tea, which they drank as they lounged by the stream. Believing they were completely alone, they made love.

They were resting near the stream when the shots came. Claudia thought the earth was exploding. She felt herself hit first in the arm, and then, as she looked up in wonder, in the neck, in the other side of her neck, in the face, in the head.[1] She was hit again and again and again, five bullets in steady succession. Blood was everywhere. Someone's terrified scream accompanied the sound of the shots. Only when Rebecca grabbed ahold of her did Claudia realize it was her own.

Rebecca said, "It's him, he's back, we have to run for cover." As they rose to flee the attack, Rebecca was hit twice, in the head and in the back. She made it to a patch of trees before crumpling to the ground.

It was late afternoon when they were sure the shooting had stopped. Claudia and Rebecca knew they had to get out of there, they had to get help. Rebecca directed Claudia to get a towel from the tent to tie around her neck like a tourniquet in order to stop the bleeding.

Rebecca could not have known that she was slowly bleeding to death from a bullet lodged in her liver. As she prepared to flee with Claudia, she realized she could not put her shoes on. She couldn't see her shoes. She couldn't stand. Claudia put Rebecca's shoes on her. She pulled Rebecca's arm around her shoulder to help support her weight, but Rebecca's legs gave way. Rebecca was wheezing, gasping for air. She was losing vision, losing speech, losing consciousness.

"It hurts," she said to Claudia, who cradled her in her arms. "Oh God, it hurts."

Claudia had to pull herself together. She knew that she had to leave Rebecca, now unconscious, and go for help. She put on a sweatshirt and sweatpants and covered Rebecca with warm things. The approaching dusk would soon become darkness. Clutching the home-made tourniquet tightly, armed with only a flashlight and a map, Claudia made her way out of the woods. She traveled nearly four miles alone, in the dark, in pain, in terror. Might her assailant be stalking her still? She didn't know.

Somehow, she reached the road. She tried to flag down a car. She looked frightened and frightening: her clothes were rumpled and blood-stained; her face was streaked with tears and dirt and blood. One car passed her by. She was determined to stop the next one. Finally, two teenaged boys stopped and carried her to the nearest town. She was then flown by helicopter to the Hershey Medical Center, where she had emergency surgery.

*   *   *

It was late when the telephone rang in my Brooklyn apartment. The only time a late night phone call is anything other than bad news is when I'm in the midst of some sort of courtship ritual. On this night, there was no sign of romance. I shoved the student exams I was grading out of the way, and picked up the receiver.

The caller asked for me by name, someone who knew me through the National Lawyers Guild suggested she contact me. She was looking for a feminist criminal lawyer who had practiced law in Pennsylvania. A close friend was in serious trouble in central Pennsylvania, near Hershey.

I was nearly finished with my first year of law teaching. Though teaching had come naturally — I liked the performance part, I liked the students, I liked the time to think — in many ways I considered myself a public defender in academic clothing. I had been a defender for five years before I took a teaching job. I took the job because it was an interesting opportunity, not because I was a burned-out defender. I loved my work and brought that enthusiasm to my teaching. My first scholarly article was on public defenders. That summer, I was going to handle a few cases for the public defender office in Philadelphia, my alma mater, and teach an evening criminal law class at a local law school.

Now, I get a fair number of calls from people in criminal trouble. The calls are usually terribly urgent and not terribly serious: someone's brother arrested for drunk driving; someone's son charged with assaulting a guy outside a bar; someone's daughter locked up on a drug charge. Though I am firmly on the defense side of criminal law practice, every now and then I get calls on behalf of victims of crime: someone's friend needs a restraining order to get an abusive husband or boyfriend out of the house; someone's sister was raped; someone's child shows signs of sexual assault.

This call was about a victim, and was both urgent and serious. There had been a shooting on the Appalachian Trail. One woman was dead and another was in critical condition in a trauma unit in central Pennsylvania, about to be questioned by a team of Pennsylvania state police officers. The women were lovers; the surviving woman was a lesbian. The police were certain to ask questions about the women's sexual identity and what they were doing before the attack. What should the surviving woman do? Should she answer the police officers' questions forthrightly? Should she leave certain things out? Should she not answer at all until she can speak to a lawyer?

I had this instinctive response from my years as a public defender: "Say nothing to the police. Tell them you're asserting your rights under *Miranda*. Tell them I'm your lawyer." There is a plainer version: "Keep your mouth shut. Wuddaya think, you're gonna talk your way outa them charging you? Jeez, and you wonder why you're always getting locked up."

But this call was not about someone being accused of committing a crime. This was a *victim*. This was someone who had been hurt. This was someone who had almost been killed. Her lover had been killed. What was she worried about? What was I worried about? Was my instinct to advise silence really about my old familiar role or was it about what it means to be a lesbian, victim or not, in central Pennsylvania, in the criminal justice system, in the world. The worry was personal.

The good lawyer in me, kind of a superego, kicked in. It was not my role to play criminal defense lawyer here, though it was my role to use the experience I had as a criminal defense lawyer to give sound advice. It was not my role to play feminist critical legal scholar here, though it was my role to use those insights to give sound advice.

The advice I gave was to tell the truth to the police, to tell it all. I told her this because when witnesses lie or distort or omit, those lies, distortions and omissions inevitably hurt them later. Good trial lawyers live for the smallest inconsistencies in police statements, defense investigative statements, pretrial testimony, and trial testimony in order to argue that the witness should not be believed. For the very same reasons that it is frightening for a lesbian to share intimate details of her life with a group of male cops, it is a bad idea to withhold those details. If she doesn't tell, the lawyer for the other side will say she's not telling still. The lawyer will say, just imagine all she's not telling. Homophobia will bolster an attack on her credibility.

The caller thanked me for the advice, and said she was looking for one more thing. She wanted to obtain a lawyer for her friend, someone who would look out for her friend's interests, not just those of the prosecution. The lawyer would be retained by the surviving victim with money raised by her friends and by the feminist and alternative communities in Ithaca, New York, where she lived. She asked me whether I was interested.

I said probably not, because, first, I wasn't sure that hiring a lawyer was such a good idea for the surviving victim, and second, if they decided to hire a lawyer, I wasn't sure it ought to be me. Lawyers representing victims in criminal court were a relatively new phenomenon.[2] Jennifer Levin's family had one — Jennifer Levin was the young woman who was killed in Central Park by Robert Chambers, "The Preppie Murderer," who eventually pleaded guilty to manslaughter — but all that lawyer seemed to do was hold the family's hand and appear at press conferences.[3]

On the other hand, I had to admit that, if ever there were a case that called out for independent counsel for a victim, this was it. Who knew what the prosecutor might be like? Who knew what political pressure might influence the handling of the case in central Pennsylvania, hardly a bedrock of social liberalism? Who knew what evidentiary issues might arise? Who knew what the jury pool was like, and what strategies might be devised by the defense to play upon a jury's homophobia and misogyny?

Still, as a criminal defense lawyer, the idea of private counsel for criminal complainants was vexing. The cards are already stacked against most criminal defendants. The last thing they need is more lawyers on the other side. Victims are witnesses for the prosecution, that's all. They are not a party in the case. These private lawyers just hover in the courtroom, constantly underfoot and in the way. They aren't a part of the record; they don't officially "appear" as counsel in the case. They're just looking for a civil case to grow out of the criminal litigation. They're looking for publicity. They're looking for money.

But if the surviving victim had made up her mind to hire someone, I understood why. So then the question was whom to hire. My view was that it would be best to hire someone local, someone who had practiced criminal law in central Pennsylvania, someone who knew the players in the court where the case would be tried. Criminal law is very parochial. Knowledge of local practice is often more important than knowledge of law.

I said I'd make some phone calls and see what names I came up with. I said I'd be in touch. I said I hoped for a speedy recovery for her friend in Hershey.

Despite some diligent phone calling, I came up with very few names. Apparently, there were very few feminist lawyers who practiced criminal law in central Pennsylvania. One prospective lawyer burst into tears upon seeing the surviving victim in her hospital room. This behavior was not helpful. It did not engender confidence.

The original caller called back. What about you, she said. It's you we want. I said okay, let's arrange for a meeting and we'll see what your friend says. If she wants me to be her lawyer, I'll do it. I was going to be in Philadelphia that summer, teaching. The case was certainly interesting. Homicides are always interesting.

In the time since the original call, the Pennsylvania police had apprehended Stephen Roy Carr and charged him with murder in the first degree of Rebecca Wight and attempted murder for the shooting of Claudia Brenner. The prosecution was seeking the death penalty.

*   *   *

When I met Claudia Brenner in June of 1988, she reminded me of me. She was around my age, Jewish, Ivy League educated, energetic. We both talked a lot. We wore the same Patagonia jacket.

I didn't cry when I saw her, or even when I heard her story. I listened. I asked questions. I wanted to know everything there was to know. I was there as a lawyer; that's the only reason I was there. I came with a legal pad, a pen, an appointments book. I told her about my background and what I envisioned my role to be in the case, painting both the worst case scenario and the best. I could be a glorified hand-holder, part tour guide, part soothsayer. I could play an active, consultative role in the prosecution.

But I was moved by Claudia, moved by the horror of her experience, moved by her courage. As a public defender, I had heard a lot of stories, a lot of terrible stories. I had questioned people who had both committed and endured acts of violence that are unimaginable to most of us. I'm also something of a criminal law junkie: I seek out crime stories in the news, in movies, on television. I figured I had pretty much heard it all.

But I hadn't. I hadn't heard this. I hadn't heard about two people innocently hiking in the woods, two people who loved each other gunned down for no reason at all. I hadn't heard about two people hanging out by a stream in the aftermath of lovemaking, who suddenly found themselves in a war zone. I hadn't sat before a woman who told me how she held her lover in her arms as she slowly and painfully bled to death.

Claudia and I got along well. We established the parameters of the lawyer-client relationship and we agreed upon a fee, something I'd never done before. Part of me felt like an imposter: What's a poverty lawyer doing charging money for legal services? Part of me felt guilty: What's a feminist lawyer doing charging money in a case like this, after all Claudia has been through? The guilty part was noisy: I can't believe you're charging poor Claudia; the honor of being asked to participate in such an important case should be compensation enough. But I also knew that the case would require an enormous amount of time and energy, and that I make my living by being a lawyer. So we settled on an amount that seemed fair to both of us.

I still wasn't sure how I felt about representing a victim, though I felt pretty good about representing Claudia. This dynamic felt familiar. I'm often more comfortable with the concrete than the abstract. I may not feel good about representing "rapists," but I almost never feel bad about representing individual clients charged with rape. I like my criminal clients, though I don't like "crime." I like the sandwich, but I don't like the ecological agony that produced the ingredients.

I was a lifelong criminal defense lawyer, and more, a public defender. I defended everyone, no matter who they were, no matter what they'd done. So long as they couldn't afford a lawyer, they had me. I became a public defender because I believed in taking sides. I believed that, especially in the criminal justice system, there were clear sides. I believed it was critically important for skilled lawyers to defend poor criminal defendants against the power of the state.

I became a public defender for all of the reasons that have ever been offered by anyone else,[4] and some of my own.[5] Being a public defender suited me. It combined irreverence and commitment, cynicism and idealism, the lure of the good fight and the sweetness of victory. Becoming a prosecutor never occurred to me. Between my politics, which started out liberal and moved steadily left through college and law school, and my personality, which aimed to please for most of my childhood and became increasingly smart-alecky as time went on, I just wasn't the type. I could speak on behalf of people but not on behalf of The People.

I had to figure out what bothered me most about being on the other side. Was it that my role was new and different and uncertain? Was it that I felt like a traitor to the criminal defense cause? Was it that I worried I would feel for the defendant, notwithstanding the crime, and feel that my place was with him?

I had to acknowledge ego. No matter what I did here — no matter how many strategies I devised, arguments I authored, witness examinations I crafted — I would be no more than a supporting player. Someone else was going to try the case. And I'm not a natural silent partner. No doubt, that's one of the reasons I decided to become a trial lawyer instead of something quieter. I worried that representing the victim was too removed a role for me. I worried that, while some of my insights might find expression in the way the case was tried, my instincts would not. Good trial lawyering involves both preparation and instinct, reading and reacting to the moment. This is nearly impossible from the sidelines.

Still, the newness was challenging. The client was appealing. The case was important. I thought I could help.

*   *   *

Stephen Roy Carr was nobody from nowhere. Though he was twenty-eight years old at the time of the shooting, he looked both younger and older, like discarded people do. Some people who kill look evil. There is a meanness in them. Other people look like sick puppies. They've been hit too many times "upside the head" to think straight anymore. Something just snaps in them. Carr was in the second group. He had been sexually and physically abused as a child. He had been on his own since he was a teenager; he was kicked out of the house or ran away. He had lived here and there.

The crime just didn't figure. Carr didn't have much of a record, and no prior violent crimes to speak of. He had spent some time in a Florida prison for grand larceny; he had stolen. He was a loner who had taken to living in the woods near the Michaux State Forest in Adams County, Pennsylvania, where the shooting occurred. He stayed on and off with old family friends, mostly going there to shower. He was closest to a teenage boy in the household, someone considerably younger than he. But he wasn't much of a talker.

After the shooting, Carr broke his rifle down, put it in a plastic garbage bag, and buried it in the ground. He also buried a knit cap he was wearing. Then he fled.

He managed to elude capture for nearly two weeks. He briefly visited the home of a family he sometimes stayed with. He told a friend that he had done a bad thing and that his rifle had been stolen. He then departed the area. He found cover and work on a farm owned by a Mennonite family; they gave him a pair of boots, and he was working to repay them. But he was apprehended because a Mennonite woman saw a composite drawing of Carr in the local newspaper, a composite Claudia had helped to construct. She called the police and told them that she believed the man they were seeking had attended her church the past Sunday.

The arrest was dramatic. Troops of armed police officers in both uniform and camouflage descended upon Carr in a barn where he was working. During his transportation to the Carlisle State Police Barracks, he talked. He talked about meeting two women on the Appalachian Trail. He said he had shot them accidentally. He thought they were deer. Then, he talked about how he didn't like the Mennonites very much. He didn't like it that the men kissed the men and the women kissed the women. Then he said he saw the two women kiss. He said he saw them have oral sex. He said if he told the truth about what happened he would be put away for a long time.

Carr took the police to the dead stump under which he had hidden the murder weapon.

*   *   *

Claudia had a lot of support. When she was hospitalized, there was always a crowd of friends in her room, hanging out in the hall, having coffee in the cafeteria. Her parents came and went; her mother was loving and concerned, but her father couldn't seem to deal with who his daughter was or what had happened to her. Her previous lover, Anne, was now best friend and family.

Several people accompanied her on every trip to Gettysburg, the county seat of Adams County and the site of the trial. The first trip was to meet the prosecutor, attend a lineup, discuss Claudia's (and my) role in decision-making, talk about scheduling, talk about initial strategy.

The prosecutor, Roy Keefer, was a nice guy, open and non-territorial. He was *the* prosecutor for the county; the only other prosecutor on staff was a part-time assistant. He took the case very seriously; this was a big case in a caseload that contained mostly small property crimes, domestic "disputes," and drunken brawls. He was remarkably unthreatened by either the case or the cast of characters. He was happy to have me participate actively in the case and to confer extensively with him; he figured two heads were better than one. This is unusual for trial lawyers, who tend to be very independent and protective of their turf. Though he didn't seem terribly worldly, he did not seem homophobic. He was a good, decent person.

We met the defense lawyer at the police station where the lineup was to be held. I had been the defense lawyer at so many lineups, it felt strange to be in this new role. I introduced myself. I wanted to say, hey, I'm usually in your shoes. Hey, I know how it feels to be the one defense lawyer in a place filled with cops and D.A.s. He was awkward and kind. He told Claudia he was sorry about what had happened to her. There wasn't much more to say.

Actually, two lineups were held: a corporeal lineup, where the witness views a line of people who generally match the description of the perpetrator; and a voice lineup, where the witness listens to several out-of-view people uttering certain words. The question is whether the witness can identify the perpetrator of the crime either visually or auditorally. Claudia identified Stephen Roy Carr immediately upon seeing him in the line. The words the voice lineup participants said were "Are you lost already?" I doubt I could identify the voice of someone who spoke to me every day, if that person were concealed from me and uttered only those few words. Claudia picked out Carr with no hesitation.

By now, the group of police officers who had been involved in the investigation of the case, and the apprehension of Carr, were founding members of the Claudia Brenner Fan Club. She was something of a local hero. Not only had she taken five bullets in her face and body and survived, not only had she hiked three miles out of the woods in the dark in that broken and bloody condition, not only had she been able to describe Carr with enough specificity to yield a composite drawing that led to his apprehension, but she had confidently and quickly identified her assailant by both his face and his voice. She was also strong, articulate, and charming. No one seemed terribly bothered by her relationship with Rebecca. No one seemed to care that she was a lesbian.

The preliminary hearing was next, coupled with a hearing on a number of pretrial matters. These included a motion to suppress the defendant's statements and the murder weapon on the grounds that they were the product of improper police questioning. There was also a lengthy discovery motion that requested, among other things, evidence of Claudia and Rebecca's sexual relationship. Apparently, we had not overestimated the role of sexuality in the case. It was clear where the defense was going.

But no amount of notice could have prepared us for what happened at the preliminary hearing. When the direct examination was concluded, defense counsel confronted Claudia with a series of cross-examination questions suggesting "provocation." Defense counsel said, you knew he was watching you, you meant to tease him, you were putting on a show, you opened up your blouses and showed him your breasts, you meant to taunt him, didn't you, didn't you, didn't you. Claudia uttered no to every question, with disbelief but dignity. She and Rebecca believed themselves completely alone.

I couldn't believe Keefer wasn't objecting. How many preliminary hearings had I participated in where the prosecutor objected to nearly every question I posed? Of all times for a prosecutor to afford the defense a meaningful opportunity for discovery in a preliminary hearing. Of all times to allow wide scope. What happened to objection, relevance? How about objection, beyond the scope of the preliminary hearing? If nothing else, what about objection, asked and answered? How many times does defense counsel get to ask plainly irrelevant, highly inflammatory, and downright insulting questions before the prosecutor complains? Maybe Keefer wasn't quick on the draw when it came to evidentiary objections, but why didn't he feel protective of his witness?

I was beside myself, stuck in the front row behind the counsel table. I wrote frantic but polite notes, not wanting to alienate the prosecutor or shed light on my true, controlling personality. I crept up to Keefer and handed him the notes once, twice, three times. More than that seemed excessive. The notes seemed to have little effect anyway. "Object," I wrote. "These questions are irrelevant to whether there is sufficient evidence to establish a prima facie case," I added. "Roy, don't you think this is getting out of hand," I pleaded. Look, he said to me later, it's a capital prosecution. I think it's fair to give some scope.

*   *   *

I couldn't fight him there. How could I fight him there? This was a capital case, a prosecution for murder in the first degree could lead to the death penalty, a death case. Of course, fairness required letting the defense do what they needed to do to mount a defense. What was I thinking, what could I have been thinking? How did I let myself get involved in this case in the first place? If ever there were an issue about which I felt deeply, about which I had always felt strongly, it is the death penalty. My opposition is unwavering.

My defense lawyer identity suddenly burst forth, like a hungry person released from a diet farm. My allegiance to the defense surfaced and reminded me that criminal defendants and criminal defense lawyers need all the friends they can get. Suddenly, I felt I should have been passing notes to the defense lawyer: don't go for broke, take small steps, establish the prior contact with the defendant on the trail, establish the contact at the first camp site, get something from the witness to suggest the defendant had a peculiar affect, get something to suggest a mental disturbance, establish that there was some nudity, establish that the defendant may have observed some sexual conduct, get what you need to get to support defendant's alarm at seeing the women intimately engaged, maybe the defendant was screaming too. Some of this might be useful in negotiating a plea or in arguing for leniency at sentencing. Some of this might lead to something less than a "murder one" conviction.

But wait. I was Claudia's lawyer, not Stephen Roy Carr's. Claudia and I had discussed the capital punishment question when we agreed to become lawyer and client. I told her I would do everything I could to help the prosecution obtain a conviction for murder in the first degree; this was a case of deliberate, premeditated murder. But I told her that I would not help the prosecution secure the death penalty. I could not support it and I could not participate in someone's execution.

Fortunately, Claudia had agreed. At the time, I mostly felt my own relief to hear that she, too, opposed the death penalty. As the case proceeded, I began to see her position as more and more remarkable. Her lover died in her arms. The guy who killed her was still walking around. Carr fired eight bullets at Claudia and Rebecca, with a single-action bolt rifle. He reloaded his weapon with each shot, and emptied his weapon after each shot. They had done nothing to him. He took his time. He fired and fired and fired. He aimed to kill.

No doubt, Claudia had conflicting thoughts about the question of punishment. Probably, there were moments when she thought Carr should pay for what he did with his life.[6] But she was always measured and reflective when she spoke about it. Execution was not the kind of vengeance she needed. She wanted Carr to understand the pain he had caused. She figured killing him wouldn't do that. She preferred that Carr be deprived of freedom for the rest of his life. She knew imprisonment would be a terrible punishment for someone who had lived out in the wild. She wanted Carr to be shunned and isolated and caged for the rest of his days. She wanted him to understand the pain. She wanted him to have to live with himself.

Moreover, there were some serious questions about the *legal relevancy* of defense counsel's questions. What did Claudia's sexual orientation, her relationship with Rebecca, an afternoon's love-making have to do with the defendant's homicidal rage as a legal matter?

*   *   *

After the preliminary hearing, and after some lawyerly soul-searching, I became convinced that the prosecution should file a motion in limine. This would prevent the defense from introducing evidence of the relationship between Claudia and Rebecca, in order to argue that Carr's murderous act was the result of provocation. The motion would prevent the defendant from cross-examining Claudia about her sexual conduct with Rebecca before the shooting, and from introducing other evidence about their sexuality. Under the facts of the case, there simply was no provocation as a matter of law.

Why did this motion require "soul-searching"? Because, the part of me that was a defense lawyer felt as I had during the preliminary hearing when I remembered that this was a capital case: disloyal and disjointed. Stephen Roy Carr had no defenses at trial: he was not insane; he was not wrongly identified; he had not acted in self-defense; he did not stumble in the woods, accidentally pulling the trigger eight times. The only defense he could raise related to the lesbian sexual relationship. Assuming I would convince the prosecutor of the soundness of my strategy, I was going to prevent the defendant from raising this defense. I was going to prevent a defendant from raising his *only* defense in a prosecution where his life was on the line.

But this was not his "only defense." This was not a defense at all. The absence of viable defenses does not give a defendant license to create one that is contrary to established law. It does not give a defendant license to create a defense that serves only to exploit the victim and inflame the jury. Under Pennsylvania law, the sort of provocation which reduces murder to manslaughter, must be "serious."[7] That does not apply to someone who intentionally kills a stranger because he doesn't like her choice of lover, or is offended by her lawful sexual conduct.[8]

A criminal defendant's "rights" are not compromised by an insistence that the defense be based on more than deep-seated bigotry. No injustice is caused by prohibiting a defense which gives legitimacy to homophobic violence. Why was I doing so much hand-wringing about proceeding with the motion? Had I, a practitioner and teacher of zealous criminal defense advocacy, reached my limit? Was I jumping ship here?

And what if I'd been the public defender in town, appointed to represent Stephen Roy Carr? Would I do it? How would I feel about it? What defenses would I raise? Would I offer the women's sexuality as relevant to my client's culpability—or to his punishment? At what cost to criminal justice? At what personal cost?

The answer is yes, I would do it. If I were the only defender in town (or one of two, as was the case in Gettysburg), the question is an easy one. The role of a public defender is to defend poor people accused of crimes, not to judge them. In view of the public hostility most criminal defendants face, and their lack of choice in counsel if they are poor, public defenders ought to be steadfast. If our clients can't choose their lawyers, why should we be able to choose our clients? The accused criminal defendant should not have to face the charges alone, whatever the nature of the charge. Soon enough, if convicted, the defendant will have to serve the sentence alone. My answer is not simply intellectual, built on my belief in the Sixth Amendment. There is a defender in my soul.

How would I feel about I? I don't know. The hypothetical may be too hypothetical. During my years as a public defender, I never felt so conflicted about representing a client that I believed the client's representation would be compromised. I have represented many clients alleged to have committed acts of hate and violence. I have represented some clients accused of bias crimes. I have represented some clients who seemed to be almost heartless. I have never felt unable to provide zealous, even empathic advocacy.[9] I believe in a high standard of criminal defense advocacy. Had I been unable to provide it, I would have withdrawn as counsel. This may be a case that pushes my personal and ideological limits. This may be a case that stirs up too much conflict for me. I don't know.

The truth is, no matter what crimes my clients are accused of committing, once I become their lawyer I feel a connection to them. No matter who they are, there is almost always something to like about them, or at least something redemptive. In this case, Claudia Brenner was my client, not Stephen Roy Carr. My allegiance was to Claudia. My heart was with her. Still, I must admit to feeling some sort of pull to the defendant here, to Claudia's attacker. I was fascinated by him. How could this skinny, woeful, barely-a-man have done this horrible, apparently deliberate act? While in jail, he had been drawing these childlike cartoons for the jail newsletter. He had drawn a Christmas card and sent it to the District Attorney. I felt haunted by these pictures. I wondered who Stephen Roy Carr was. What was going on in his head? What had his life been like? What led him to the moment of the shooting?[10] I sometimes even worried about the quality of his representation.

I suppose the harder question is whether, if I were one of many public defenders or court-appointed counsel available, and I had a choice in the cases I took, I would represent Stephen Roy Carr. I probably would. I don't think I would go out of my way to get myself appointed to this case, but I don't think I'd turn it down either.

I would not use the victims' sexuality as part of any substantive defense, such as provocation; it is irrelevant. I admit that I also find this defense deeply offensive — but, more importantly, I believe that many jurors would share my reaction. My decision would be legal and tactical. If observing women engaging in lawful, consensual sexual conduct sparked some sort of mental impairment in the defendant, such as temporary insanity or diminished capacity, and I had the evidence to support this assertion, I would raise it. If there was something about encountering the women lovers that related to something in the defendant's background which mitigated his culpability, I would absolutely raise it at sentencing.

My view is that there would be a cost to criminal justice if lawyers like me refused as a group to represent defendants like Stephen Roy Carr. As to personal cost, I suppose there might be some if I *only* represented the Stephen Roy Carrs of the world. But I don't.

*   *   *

At the hearing on the motion in limine, which I wrote and the prosecutor argued, the defense added a novel argument to their opposition. They argued that the defendant ought to be able to introduce evidence of his personal history to support the defense of provocation. His offer of proof included the following: he had been sexually abused as a child; he had been sexually assaulted by a man in prison; his mother "may be involved in a lesbian relationship," he was ridiculed at school and made to take showers there; he had been rejected by women his entire life.[11]

The offer of proof defied both credibility and the reasonable person standard, which is at the core of legally adequate provocation. Carr was sexually abused and assaulted? He and how many others? His mother "may" be a lesbian? What are we talking about here? Is there a rumor in the neighborhood? Did someone see Carr's mother in a gay bar? And what if his mother *is* a lesbian? He had been rejected by women his whole life? Now, there's a frightening defense to murder.

The motion in limine was successful. Who could have predicted that the presiding judge would understand the issue well enough to write the following:

> [The women] sought the solitudes of a location thought pristine. Many may frown upon what they did, but they broke no law and only pursued activities in which they had a right to engage.
>
> Defendant, on the other hand, brought an attitude and disposition that would be considered evil in any civilized circumstance.
>
> People seem to live constantly in eras when one group or another feel justified in ending human life for reasons thought to be sufficient. History is replete with examples of utmost cruelty being inflicted on those termed heretic, witches, sodomites and the like. . . .
>
> [T]here was no relationship between the victims and Defendant. The victims . . . did not harm Defendant. . . . His murderous act cannot be mitigated by such trivial provocation.[12]

*   *   *

On the eve of trial, the defendant decided to plead guilty to murder in the first degree in exchange for a sentence of life in prison without the possibility of parole. The plea was the result of the motion in limine, the absence of any meaningful defense to the charges, and the defendant's fear of the death penalty.

Claudia was relieved; as she had hoped, Carr would be convicted of nothing less than murder in the first degree. Carr had committed the most serious crime under law, and nothing about her relationship with Rebecca lessened his crime. Notwithstanding her experience at the preliminary hearing, she had mixed feelings about the loss of her "day in court." We had prepared well, and she was ready. The plea was, no doubt, an anti-climax.

Rebecca's father was less accepting of the plea negotiation. He wanted Carr executed. He did not mince words. He had no ambivalence about how Carr should be punished. He would not feel "whole" if Carr was merely sent away forever.

Claudia never expected the criminal system to make her whole. Something had been taken from her that could never be replaced.

Nor was the healing process going to take place in a criminal court-room.

*   *   *

Today, Claudia is fully recovered from her physical injuries, lives with friends in a house in the country, and practices architecture in Ithaca, New York. She speaks frequently on hate crimes and violence against lesbians and gays.

As for me, I have become a criminal lawyer and teacher who writes and talks a lot about personal and professional conflict in the practice of criminal law. I am interested in the complexities of professional role, in the demands of personal conscience.

Life looks a little different to me now, more paradoxical, more grey. While I still believe in picking sides, and I remain convinced that there are sides to pick, the picking is tougher.

I know I met a hero back in the summer of 1988. I have never met anyone quite like Claudia. I know that I was profoundly affected by serving as her lawyer. There are some cases that spill out into life. Sometimes I think I get more from my clients than I give. More than anything else, this essay is a tribute to courage, to unbending belief in self, and to Claudia Brenner.

NOTES

[1]See Claudia Brenner, *Survivor's Story: Eight Bullets*, in Gregory M. Herek and Kevin T. Berril, *Hate Crimes: Confronting Violence Aagainst Lesbians and Gay Men* (1992).

[2]See generally, Ellen Yaroshefsky, "Balancing Victim's Rights and Vigorous Advocacy for the Defendant," 1989 *Annual Survey of American Law 135.*

[3]See, e.g., Vivian Berger, "It's the State, Not the Family, vs. Chambers", *Newsday*, March 9, 1988, at 62. It is interesting to note that the recent spate of highly publicized cases where criminal complainants hired their own lawyers almost always involve women and sex. After Jennifer Levin, there was Patricia Bowman, who accused William Kennedy Smith of raping her in Palm Beach in 1991, and Desiree Washington, who accused Mike Tyson of raping her in Indianapolis the same year. Both had private lawyers representing them throughout the course of the criminal proceedings.

[4]See Barbara Babcock, "Defending the Guilty", 32 *Cleveland State Law Review* 175, 177–79 (1983–84) (citing the "garbage collector's reason," the "legalistic or positivist's reason," the "political activist's reason," the "social worker's reason," the "egotist's reason."); Seymour Wishman, "A Criminal Lawyer's Inner Damage," *Minneapolis Tribune*, July 23, 1977, at 6A (" . . . everyone is entitled to the best defense, . . . ego gratification, the joys of good craftsmanship, the need to make a living, the

desire to minimize the length of inhumane treatment of those convicted, and after all, some of my clients may be innocent.").

[5]See Abbe Smith, "Rosie O'Neill Goes to Law School: The Clinical Education of a Sensitive, New Age Public Defender", 28 *Harvard C.R.-C.L. L. Review* 1 (1993) ("I like my clients, I like the work, something funny happens every day, something poignant happens every day, and I saw *To Kill a Mockingbird* too many times as an impressionable child. As far as I'm concerned, there are no two more joyful words in the English language than the words 'not guilty.' ").

[6]See Susan Jacoby, *Wild Justice: The Evolution Of Revenge* (1983) (quoting Albert Camus' essay, "Reflections on the Guillotine," in which he explained that his opposition to the death penalty was not based on an illusion about the natural goodness of human beings: "I do not believe . . . that there is no responsibility in this world and that we must give way to that modern tendency to absolve everyone, victim and murderer, in the same confusion.").

[7]18 Pa. C.S.A. s2503(a)(1)(2).

[8]See Commonwealth vs. Cisneros, 381 Pa. 447, 451, 113 A.2d 293, 296 (1955) ("The law of Pennsylvania is clear that no words of provocation, reproach, abuse or slight assault are sufficient to free the party from guilt of murder."); Commonwealth v. Bonadio, 490 Pa. 91, 415 A.2d 47 (1980) (holding that it is not unlawful for consenting adults to engage in sexual conduct with a member of the same sex in Pennsylvania). See also Commonwealth v. Long, 460 Pa. 461, 333 A.2d 865 (1975); Commonwealth v. McCusker, 460 Pa. 382, 292 A.2d 286 (1972); Commonwealth v. Colandro, 231 Pa. 343, 80 A. 571 (1911).

[9]See generally Charles J. Ogletree, Jr., "Beyond Justifications: Seeking Motivations to Sustain Public Defenders", 106 *Harvard Law Review*. 1239 (1993).

[10]See generally Abbe Smith, "Criminal Responsibility, Social Responsibility", and "Angry Young Men: Reflections of a Feminist Criminal Defense Lawyer", *New York University Review Law & Social Change* (forthcoming June 1994).

[11]See *Commonwealth v. Stephen Roy Carr*, No. CC-385–88, Court of Common Pleas, Adams County, Pennsylvania, *Opinion on Post-Verdict Motions*, Oscar F. Spicer, President Judge, at 3–4 [hereinafter *Opinion on Post-Verdict Motions*].

[12]*Opinion on Post-Verdict Motions*, supra note 14, at 13, 16. See also Commonwealth vs. Stephen Roy Carr, 398 Pa. Super. 306, 308, 310, 580 A.2d 1362, 1363, 1364 (1990) ("[T]he principle issue is whether the trial court erred when it disallowed evidence of the defendant's psychosexual history to show the likelihood of a killing in the heat of passion aroused by defendant's observation of two women engaged in . . . lovemaking. . . . The sight of naked women engaged in lesbian lovemaking is not adequate provocation to reduce an unlawful killing from murder to voluntary manslaughter. It is not an event which is sufficient to cause a reasonable person to become so impassioned as to be incapable of cool reflection. A reasonable person would simply have discontinued his observation and left the scene; he would not kill the lovers."); Commonwealth vs. Stephen Roy Carr, Pa., A.2d (1991) (allocatur denied).

ROBERT FEKETY

GENESIS II
A Parable for the 21st Century About Gene Transfer Therapy

$\mathfrak{I}$n the beginning, God created the heavens and the earth, and
also the DNA.

And a spring rose out of the earth and watered its surface.

Then from the earth's dust and slime, from its nucleic acids,
proteins and sugars, the Lord God formed a man.

And He breathed into the man's face the breath of life and the
likeness of God.

And the man became a living soul called Adam.

And then the Lord God planted a Paradise of pleasure, wherein
He placed the man to dress it and to keep it.

And the Lord God brought forth from the ground in the midst of
Paradise all manner of trees, fair to behold and pleasant to
eat of; also the Tree of Knowledge of DNA and the Tree of
Life.

And He commanded Adam, saying: Of every tree of Paradise
thou shalt eat,

But of the Tree of Knowledge of DNA thou shalt not eat.

For in that day when thou shalt eat of it, thou shalt die the
Death.

$\mathcal{A}$nd then the Lord God said: It is not good for man to be
alone;

Let Us make him a being like unto himself.

And the Lord God formed out of the slime and the DNA all the
beasts of the earth and the fowl of the air,

But for Adam there was still not one like himself.

So the Lord God cast a deep sleep upon Adam,

And then He drew bone marrow out of one of the man's ribs, and
gathered chromosomes from it,

And the Lord God chose two chromosomes that were like crosses,
and more than two score others, also some bearing genes for
beauty and wisdom.

And the Lord God gathered up the chromosomes, the genes, the
DNA and their proteins and fashioned them into a woman,
and He brought her to Adam.

And Adam said: This now is DNA of my DNA, and flesh of my
flesh, and he named the woman Eve, and cleaved to her as
his wife.

And both Adam and Eve were naked, but they were not
ashamed.

And then God saw all the things that He had made, and they
were good.

So on the seventh day God ended His work and He rested.

Now the DNA of the serpent was more cunning than the DNA
of all the beasts of the earth the Lord God had made.

And the serpent said to the woman: Why hath God commanded
you, that you should not eat of every tree of Paradise?

And the woman answered him, saying: Of the fruit of many trees
that are in Paradise we do eat,

But of the fruit of the Tree of Knowledge of DNA in the midst of
Paradise, God hath commanded us that we should not touch
it or eat its fruit, lest perhaps we become infected with Evil
DNA and die.

And the serpent said to the woman: No, you shall not die the
Death.

For God doth know that in that day when you shalt eat the DNA
thereof, your eyes shall be opened, and you shall be as God,
knowing Good and Evil;

And you shall know neither fear, hunger, ignorance, sickness,
suffering, sadness nor want.

And you shall live forever.

And then Adam and Eve saw that the DNA of the Tree of
Knowledge was fair to the eyes and delightful to behold.

And in the year one thousand nine hundred and fifty-three they took the DNA thereof and did eat.*

And their eyes were opened and they perceived themselves to be naked, and they were afraid.

And when they heard the Voice of the Lord God walking in Paradise in the afternoon air, Adam and Eve hid themselves amidst the trees of Paradise.

And the Lord God called to Adam and said: Where art thou?

And Adam said: I hid myself when I heard Thy Voice in Paradise, because I was naked, and I was mournful and afraid.

And the Lord God said to him: And who hath told thee that thou wast naked?

For unless thou hast eaten of the Tree whereof I commanded thee that thou shouldst not eat, lest thou become infected with Evil DNA, you would not know this.

And Adam said: the serpent deceived us, and so the woman and I did eat that which Thou said we should not, and now we are hungry and know not what to do.

And the Lord God said to the serpent: Because thou hast done this evil thing, thou art cursed among all the beasts of the earth:

I will put enmities between your DNA and the DNA of the woman; thou shalt crawl upon thy breast and lie in wait for her heel, and she shall crush thy head.

And to Adam God said: Because thou hast hearkened to the serpent and eaten the Fruit of the Tree whereof I commanded thee that thou shouldst not eat, thy DNA has been tainted, and the earth is cursed in thy work: with labor and toil and the sweat of thy face thou shalt bring forth thorns and thistles and eat bread all the days of thy life, till thou return to the earth out of which thou wast taken. For dust thou art, and unto dust thou shalt return.

To the woman Eve He said: Because thou hast done this thing,

---

*J. D.Watson, F. H. C. Crick. "Molecular structure of nucleic acids. A structure for deoxyribose nucleic acid." *Nature* 1953; 171:737–38. "Genetical implications of the structure of deoxyribose nucleic acid." *Nature* 1953; 171:964–67.

thou shalt be cursed under thy husband's power and
dominion: Your conceptions will multiply your sorrows, and
your DNA coupled with that of your husband is cursed, and
shalt at times bring forth tainted and troubled children.
And the Lord God made for Adam and Eve garments of skins,
and He clothed them, but they were still afraid and
ashamed.

And then the Lord God said to The Spirit: Behold, Adam and
Eve have become as one of Us, knowing Good from Evil:
Now, therefore, lest perhaps they put forth their hand and take
more Evil DNA, or the DNA of the Tree of Life, so as to live
forever:
We will send them out of Paradise, to till the earth from which
they were taken, and their days shall be numbered.
So the Lord God cast Adam and Eve out of Paradise, and He
placed a flaming sword before the Tree of Life to shield it.
And God said: My spirit shall not remain in men and women
forever, because they are flesh, and their days shall be a
hundred and twenty years.

And then Adam and Eve begot sons and daughters, and soon
myriads of men and women were multiplied upon the earth.
And some of them were gifted and clever, and they began to use
Good DNA to overcome diseases and other afflictions in
beings tainted with Evil DNA.
And the Lord God was pleased.
But in time God saw that the wickedness of men and women was
great, for the hearts of some of them desired the DNA of the
Tree of Life, and they also conspired to use Good DNA in
evil ways, and even to make all persons like unto themselves.
And He saw also that they used DNA greedily and in hatred.
And when He saw that they were using DNA to rid the earth of
traits of other races, and of traits they envied but could not
have for themselves, He regretted that He had made man
and woman on the earth.
And being touched inwardly with sorrow of heart,
He said: I will destroy man and woman, whom I have created,
from the face of the earth, and also the beasts and the fowl,
and all other living creatures.

So, in the third millennium, in the seven hundredth year of the life of Aaron, in the third month, on the seventh day of the month, all the fountains of the great deep were broken up, and the flood gates of heaven were opened.

And once again rain fell upon the earth for forty days and forty nights, and the winds and the seas trumpeted their great strength.

And all things on the earth wherein there was the breath of life died.

But Aaron had found grace before The Spirit, the Mother of Wisdom and Holiness, for he had done all things which She had commanded him, and Aaron and his wife had not coveted Evil DNA or the Tree of Life in the Paradise of pleasure.

So The Spirit told Aaron to build a spacecraft of titanium and samarium within and without.

And Aaron and his wife and all their creatures went into the spacecraft, and they rose up into the heavens and remained safe above the raging floods and howling winds.

And then the waters receded, and The Spirit of Wisdom smelled a sweet savour, and She said:

We must no longer curse the earth because of men and women, for their inspirations and the thoughts of their hearts are no longer prone to Evil:

And all the days of the earth, summer and winter, night and day, shall not cease.

And She spoke to Aaron, saying: Go out of thy craft, thou and thy wife, and those that are with thee of all flesh:

Go forth upon the earth and love all thy neighbors:

Sow DNA amongst them with everlasting wisdom and prudence, and thou shalt overcome the suffering of men and women of all races.

And then God the Father and Mother gave their blessing and love to Aaron and his wife, their sons and daughters and all the creatures,

And They said to them: Go now and fill the earth with happy, healthy children.

S. BEN-TOV

HEREDITY

Adam and Eve, at Stanford's
Human Genome Conference
separated onstage. Footlights
glazed the trellised ivy
flanking their black platform;
the backdrop, a movie screen
on which Adam projected slides.
Stage left: his pinkish cannonball
bespectacled, his magisterial
spiel squealing with feed-
back, his reflective papers
on the halogen-lit lectern.
Stage right: Eve, revealed in full
dress, an inflight stewardess
charmingly miming safety
procedures — she interpreted
for the deaf. Groomed leaves
brushed her neutral calves.

Adam displayed a chromosome,
squiggling with the future
endowments of drosophila,
and he named some genes.
Unlike the fruit-fly's, human
genetic material's details
are infinitely difficult of access.
(The hushed hall relished
our secret gifts.) Technically described,
the procedures directed
at deciphering us, stupefy

even research foundation boards;
despite recombinant DNA's
delivering the private sector
its heaven-sent ladder. Next slide.
Here is our problem: (a caricature
of melted structural girders.
An ICBM — black arrow —
slid around, smoothly panicked.
No, no.) A signless roadmap
of continental interstates. The X'ed
California town was where
Adam lost his wallet. Imagine
him retracing his footsteps
from, say, Massachusetts, searching
I-90 for that wallet: one human gene.

Squinting at what Adam lost
as futilely as doomed
balloons bob along a ceiling,
the auditorium of heads
nodded. Translating Adam,
Eve's quick gestures loosed
filaments of immediate past.
Her hands loomed air
to patterned gossamer,
fabricating space and time,
and the material identical
to both, impassioned dream;
as I search my mirrored eyes
to see again my father's
clear thread doubling back,
an emerging figure. Adam,
the translation ran, was lost.
He stole along dark roads.
I had no questions afterwards,
when screen, lectern, plants,
Adam, Eve, and descendants
left not a rack behind. I'd lost,
now remembering to regret,
the small scab, like flaked gold,

my father stored in a cottonball
among his eyeglass screws
and watchsprings, till he died:
the snipped cord of my birth —
my question is why my loose
end ended in those clear cells —
his miniature plastic drawers
where circuit chips, resistors,
left- and right-threaded screws
like sutras, readied to connect
his laboratory's microcosm?
What did the inventor make
of fatherhood?

Like a marvelous griffon,
he bent his tufted brows,
and his eyelids, over a gleam,
tightened at their corners;
one hand wrote, the other beat
a tattoo upon an inch of air.
His notebook, brown as horn,
opened to fine ballpoint
illuminated mechanisms
his script flew past. Behind,
one thousand reagent bottles
shelved the laboratory walls
opposite continuous windows
filled with thin birches'
interlaced frost, or green light.
Machines freighted worktables:
smooth serpentining cables
choked the outlets; alligator
clips' petty jaws bit sparks;
a transformer uttered a bass
twangle, ignored by monitors.
A stylus traced the world's
teeth on spooling tape. Where
a bench sweated solder, the small
plastic chest pearled it over
wracked scrap-metal. I. Ben-Tov

devised what he lived from daily,
ranging around this jumble,
singing, to the pegboard wall's
hand power tools, heraldic Black
& Decker, charged with orange,
each sawblade a chrome shudder.
Lathe and sander stood on trestles,
while metaphysical engines
hovered just beyond reach,
turning ideas out of nothing.
Telephones jarred; a receiver rode
his shoulder like a bold crow.
He stooped over his lathe's
hum, scream and steel shavings'
geranium order (oh my bright
childish fistfuls!). He broke off
singing, and raised a silk-
finished component to the light.

When death froze the nerve
of his laboratory, and blacked
the clear windows, not knowing
where to look among the self-
absorbed objects, I sat down
and powered the oscilloscope.
A blip raced. A green line
rose and fell like wavy rope,
caracoled like coiling vines
or helical DNA; a spell wound
around time's wound. Hurt
to be enthralled, I looked
outside. Birches in beckoning leaf.
A shunting of the frame, some
shift of genetic code-triplets,
warp-strands raised or lowered,
and the shuttle, holy boat, shot
laced birches or a woman
through the web that animates
its loom. All daughterhood
or fatherhood meant was thrall

to the fabrication of our parts.
Yet, discovering whom I lost—
that loose end of my being
he treasured as if for use—
I dreamed heredity was love.

ENRICO MARIO SANTÍ

UNBURNT BRIDGES: AN ESSAY ON CUBA

para María Elena Cruz Varela

*This essay is a revised version of the paper I read at the conference
"Cuba at the Crossroads: The Future of Democracy in Cuba," sponsored by the James Dickey Center for International Understanding
at Dartmouth College, Hanover, New Hampshire, February 19–21,
1995.*

*One reference requires some prior explanation. The first session of
the conference featured two well-known leaders from the Cuban-
American community: Eloy Gutiérrez Menoyo, President of "Cam-
bio Cubano," an exile political organization that advocates dialogue
and negotiation with the Castro regime, and María Elena Cruz
Varela, the Cuban poet who until one year ago headed "Criterio
Alternativo," a human rights opposition group in Cuba. Cruz Varela
left Havana nine months ago and currently lives in Puerto Rico.
After their two speeches, and as soon as the question and answer
session opened, I happened to ask the first question of Mr. Gutiérrez
Menoyo. Mine was a two-part query. First, in relation to his recent
meeting in Spain with Roberto Robaina, the Cuban Minister of
Foreign Relations, which reportedly had discussed the opening of
political space for the opposition in Cuba, I asked whether he could
fill us in on his discussions with Robaina on such prospects. Second,
how did Gutiérrez Menoyo respond to the critiques hurled at him,
Ramón Cernuda, and Alfredo Durán, the other exile leaders who
had participated in the meeting with Robaina in Spain, for joining
in a discussion which had left out other broadly-based exile organizations, like the Cuban-American National Foundation?*

*Gutiérrez Menoyo became visibly upset with my second question,
so much so that he bypassed my first question. He went on to scold*

me, screaming, all the while pointing his index finger at me, for worrying about an organization (the CANF) that systematically excluded him from public discussions of the Cuba issue in Miami, where he lived, and persecuted him with placard-carrying members at conferences such as the one we were attending. After Gutiérrez Menoyo had finished his tirade against me, which lasted a good ten minutes, many in the audience, including many of the scholars who had been invited as speakers, applauded him approvingly. None so much as stood up to criticize his attitude, which deserves to be called authoritarian and non-democratic, to say the least. Nor did I choose to stand up and rebut him, as did a couple of Cuban-Americans from the audience whom I had never met. I chose instead to delay my reply until I got my turn to address the conference two days later. What I read then is contained in Part I. To it I have now added further reflections that have crystallized since the conference took place.

Part II is an extended quotation of statements made by Osvaldo Payá and Gustavo Arcos, two leaders of prominent human rights organizations in Cuba, which were taped in Havana in early 1994 and smuggled out in a five-minute video. The video, which was played to the conference as part of my address, was graciously provided to me by my friend Frank Calzón, Director of the Washington-based Freedom House, a human rights watch organization.

Part III is a text I wrote in Spanish and published in Vuelta *(Mexico City) last summer, in the wake of the August 1994 uprising in Havana which led to the rafters' crisis and exodus shortly thereafter. I included it as part of my address, and include it now, because to date it has not lost its currency or relevance, unfortunately.*

FROM HANOVER TO HAVANA

Flashback. Late fall 1979. Hanover, New Hampshire. Three friends of mine in the Dartmouth Spanish department hastily organize a meeting on Cuba at a campus retreat nearby and ask me to participate. The occasion is the visit to Dartmouth of Cuban novelist Edmundo Desnoes, author of the novel and film *Memories of Underdevelopment*, and the visit to the United States of Miguel

Barnet, author of *Autobiography of a Runaway Slave* and other testimonial novels. I come to Dartmouth and meet with my friends. It's an in-house retreat, so no townees are allowed, only Dartmouth faculty and some others, like me, from other universities. Present at the retreat also was Carollee Bengelsdorf, who was then married to Desnoes and a political scientist in her own right. Present as well was Lourdes Casal, a powerful presence in the lives of young Cuban exiles then, someone with whom we were, in our own way, "building bridges" to Cuba.

The context for my visit to Dartmouth was, however, equivocal. With Lourdes, and another some thirty Cuban exile academics, I had traveled to Cuba during the previous summer. It was my second visit. The year before, in late 1978, I had formed part of the motley contingent of Cubans everywhere known as *el diálogo* which had traveled to Havana in order to facilitate, among other things, the amnesty of political prisoners and the reunification of families. Like those hundreds of Cubans, I too dreamed of building a solid bridge which I dared to cross, despite the protestations of my parents and many friends. My three-day trip to Havana in 1978 had been too brief, my enthusiasm too contained, in order not to repeat it. So, the following year I went again, this time for two weeks, on a trip sponsored by *Areíto*, a journal and group that we all believed in then (though I had turned down an invitation to become a member of its board.)

I had come to Dartmouth, then, as (what I perceive now) an ideologically safe guest. No title for my talk had been demanded before our meeting, but I decided to speak on Heberto Padilla, the dissident poet who had been punished by the Cuban government almost a decade before, and whose latest poems (now collected in his *Autobiography of the Other*) had just appeared the previous week in *The New York Review of Books*. I felt then that those poems deserved a review of their own. But my position was ambivalent because after my second trip to Cuba my views on the Cuban Revolution had changed.

Whereas my first trip had been sponsored by the Cuban government — complete with a single room at the Hotel Riviera (built by the Mafia in the fifties it was still then one of Havana's swankiest), a chauffeur, a so-called guide to drive me wherever I wanted, and even a celebration night at Tropicana, my second trip had resulted in a sad, and until then secret, disillusionment. In my travels from one end of the island to the other, I had met many desperate people—some of them begging for dollars that could help them buy a pair of shoes at the *diplotienda*, or diplomatic shop, others simply curious to learn how a Polaroid camera worked. But the most desperate of all had been my uncle Agustín, who then lived and still lives in the same home in Santiago with his family and who had spent fifteen years as a political prisoner in the Isle of Pines. For complex family reasons, my uncle had decided the previous year to turn down my offer to help him negotiate his departure from Cuba along with the thousands of other political prisoners. Now I sensed that his desperation was not material but spiritual and emotional: despite my interest in his personal story and my repeated desire to know how he felt about his life, we remained alienated from one another. He never revealed anything, and communication was difficult. I suspect that he suspected me: twice I had been invited by the government, there I was asking him about his life and whether he was happy, all the while he had spent fifteen years in prison and all that his family had been able to offer me that morning for breakfast had been a glass of water and one *tostón*, a piece of fried plantain. To top things off, I even wore a beard. But such was the dignified nobility of my family, and of my uncle Agustín in particular, that, unlike many of the strangers I had met throughout the island, never once did they complain about their situation.

Many other things happened to make those two weeks in 1979 the summer of my discontent. But it had been my uncle's empty gaze, rather than the empty pockets that he and many other Cubans I had met had shown me—pockets, I might add, that were grotesquely similar to the ones I had seen elsewhere in Latin America, in Mexico City or in San Juan—that had changed me inside. Inside, that is, because I had not dared to speak out and criticize what I had seen. I couldn't, because I felt trapped. Upon returning from Havana after my first trip in 1978, I along with a number of participants in the *diálogo* had begun receiving death threats from right-wing Cuban exile paramilitary groups, like Alpha 66, in pursuit of vengeance for our having crossed the bridge to Havana. That same December, for example, I received from them a list of crossed-out names of people whom Alpha 66 had either killed or maimed with letter bombs and which contained mine, about to be crossed out and adorned with the gentle message, like a Spanish Hallmark Christmas Card: TE TENEMOS EN CUENTA, we're keeping you in mind.

I hadn't dared to speak, then, until I showed up in Hanover that fateful evening in the first week of December of 1979 hoping to have my friends listen to me through the oblique allegory of Padilla's prison poems. My distribution and explication of those texts was met with indifference by some and with fury by others. Both Edmundo and Carol, I seem (or at least would like) to recall, rushed to my defense after Lourdes and Barnet—more shocked at my daring gesture to have brought the texts of the apostate than indignant at the subject itself—questioned my entire presentation as provocative and irrelevant. When the debate was over, and it seemed to me then to last forever, I felt an overwhelming sense of emptiness. I had come to Dartmouth seeking validation from my friends for my doubts, but instead had met a silent, albeit equally as damaging, letter bomb.

Later that same month, I took that emptiness with me to Tampa, Florida, for the first research leave of my academic career, where I was to live for the next several months finishing a book. Near enough to a Cuban community though safely distant from Miami, I used to think. It was there that I learned again that there's no escaping from oneself. May of 1980, like August 1994, was a fateful month of the Cuban diaspora that brought to the Florida shores not only the mental patients whom I saw escorted in bulging buses across my Tampa neighborhood, but entire destitute families, uncannily similar to the ones I had met and seen throughout my travels in Cuba the year before, families like my uncle Agustín's. I also met young Cuban writers and intellectuals, like Reinaldo Arenas, with whom I soon became close friends, who in my two trips to Cuba had remained off-limits to inquiring scholars like me because of his so-called unspeakable crimes and whom I finally interviewed that month of May 1980 in an anonymous apartment in the northwest section of Little Havana. For me the Mariel boatlift had brought down, had undone, the *diálogo*. The *diálogo* had brought out political prisoners, but not everyone wanted to or could leave; and the boatlift definitely questioned such widely-advertised policies as "family reunification," which we as a group had worked so idealistically to achieve.

Since 1980 the sense of double (or triple) exile I felt has become one of the fundamental elements of my writing. If I was already a political exile from both Cuba and the exile community—a CIA agent in Cuba and the G-2 [the Cuban Security Police] in Miami—I have also become a spiritual exile by virtue of being a writer and intellectual who criticizes equally the regime and the inactive (perhaps reactive) U.S. policy toward Cuba. Eventually, the yearly greetings from Alpha 66 stopped coming, but in 1986, in reaction to an essay of mine on "José Martí and the Cuban Revolution," a keynote address at a UCLA conference on Cuba, I was attacked twice in Havana intellectual journals and called everything from "lost" and "man without a country" to "a servant of imperialist interests" to "racist"—the latter an accusation that would of course have shocked my ancestors from Santiago de Cuba. To top things off, that same year and using the same essay on Martí as an excuse, a certain Cuban writer decided to make an example of me by accusing me, in a public polemic with Professor Arcadio Díaz Quiñones, of having become, along with none other than Octavio Paz and even the late Angel Rama—a Uruguayan intellectual of the Left—an "ideologue of the Cuban exile community." My repeated requests to reply to these accusations were never answered.

Flash forward. It was with this personal background that I accepted the invitation to return to Hanover to discuss once again the subject of Cuba. It's hard to believe that sixteen years have gone by. Edmundo and Carol are no longer together; Lourdes Casal and Reinaldo Arenas have died; Antonio Benítez Rojo, my host at Casa de las Américas in Havana when I visited in 1979, has since defected and was an invited participant in this symposium. So was Marifeli Pérez-Stable, one of the leaders of Areíto, whose political views have changed considerably; Eloy Gutiérrez Menoyo, who in 1978 headed the list of political prisoners we discussed as part of the *diálogo*, was one of the two keynote speakers. And yet, although so much has gone by, why did I feel the same emptiness that I felt on that December night of 1979 as soon as Gutiérrez Menoyo, pointing his finger at me, answered my question on the possibility of opening up political spaces for the opposition in Cuba in a manner that, while perhaps personally justified, was nevertheless undemocratic, not to say unkind? After the session I walked up to Gutiérrez Menoyo, and shook his hand. I tried to show him no bitterness and gave him a capsule summary of the personal story I just told you. Gutiérrez Menoyo is a noble man, a former political prisoner, like my uncle Agustín, so he apologized for having spoken to me defensively, after years of harassment by his political adversaries in Miami. I'm not worried about him, though. I'm only worried about those who applauded him for pointing his finger at me.

I have been, as far back as I can remember, politically incorrect. The emptiness I felt both times at Hanover goes back to the way I used to feel between the ages of ten and twelve, during my last two years living in Cuba, growing up in a home where views against the Castro regime were openly discussed but were kept away from neighbors and friends, and even some close relatives like my uncle Agustín, then a raving revolutionary. It was then that I first had the epithet of *gusano* — the Cuban version of the German *Ungeziefer*, with which Dr. Goebbels, borrowing from Kafka, had referred to Jews and intellectuals — hurled at me. Today, as I read about efforts to build bridges to Cuba, like the recent two-volume issue of *Michigan Quarterly Review* (Summer and Fall 1994), I worry and am saddened about the possible recurrence of the manipulation and naive political stands to which I once fell victim. I have no reason to doubt the good will that permeates such enterprises. All of us Cubans need to believe in the possibility of national redemption, in the achievement of reconciliation between the two halves of the Cuban nation torn asunder by thirty-six years of dictatorship. But then why not recognize as well the need to build a bridge with support *on both sides*, as any cautious engineer would, and plead for a commensurate opening on the island side of the Florida straits?

The space that makes such reconciliation possible, the structure that would make the bridge work, has a name: Democracy. Democracy was the word contained in the cries of freedom screamed by rioting Cubans on August 4, 1994, and yet it is the word missing most glaringly from the two-volume issue of MQR. Why such reluctance to talk about the need for democracy among Cubans — not just in the island, but in exile as well? Democracy is the undergirding that would support any bridge to Cuba; but the democratic imagination is precisely what is muted in the multi-voiced chorus appearing in the two volumes, particularly at those points where one would expect to hear it most clearly.

At the head of the Introduction to Part One of "Bridges to Cuba," for example, the editors quote, almost as if it were their guiding motto, the final lines of the poem "Un puente, un gran puente," [A Bridge, a Large Bridge], by the great Cuban poet José Lezama Lima:

> A bridge, a great bridge, which can't be seen,
> its boiling, frozen waters
> batter against the last defensive walls. . . .

But the stanza from which these lines are quoted goes on for four more lines, lines which resonate loudly and prophetically (Lezama Lima died in 1976, the victim of a cruel internal exile) and bespeak the need to enlist a pluralist and democratic imagination against the transparent tropes of a common authoritarian enemy. They read:

and they steal the head, and the single voice
crosses the river again, like the blind king
who does not know he's been dethroned
and he dies stitched softly to fidelity at night.

FROM HAVANA TO HANOVER (TWO VOICES)

Osvaldo Payá: We, as Cubans, defend our sovereignty. We believe that we should resolve our problems as Cubans and among Cubans. We appreciate the deep concern and great international solidarity toward the Cuban people. However, we cannot fail to realize that there are international factors which throughout history have made Cuba the object of confrontations, such as the East-West conflict, and which often saw the spilling of Cuban blood in places far from our soil.

Today, the confrontation has opened onto a new international relationship. However, our country is stalled under the signs of a confrontation which is amplified but which also has its basis in reality. I refer, with all deliberation, to the situation of U.S. policy toward Cuba. For many, that is the crux of the Cuban problem. And yet the crux of the Cuban problem is not that. Its essence is rather the political and economic marginalization that the Cuban people are enduring today.

One hears talk about Cuba's right to self-determination. There are two sides to this issue. One is the Cuban people's self-determination as a nation, as a country. The other is self-determination as the Cuban people's right to determine its own destiny, to elect its own government, to design by itself and according to its own circumstances the model of social justice which we will find among all of us. And among all of us means through a national dialogue. Therefore, Cuba's most fundamental problem today, when we speak of self-determination, is one of looking at reality and realizing that what our people lack is precisely the right to self-determination due to the lack of freedom in our own country.

Gustavo Arcos: With the victory of what was once known as a democratic, nationalist revolution in 1959 (everyone knows what happened later, so there's no need to explain), it became very sad that the entire history of a people, of millions of lives, became influenced by one individual who, either due to his charisma or other factors, should have become the undisputed arbiter of the country's destiny. He is a man with many qualities. But now we can pass judgment and everyone agrees that he had two major character flaws. First, an unhealthy political ambition, a greed for power above everything else. Second, that later he showed, despite his Catholic education—and one assumes that all believers protect themselves against evil, against base passions, through their education—that he was totally amoral. He was not a Communist, but in order to retain power, in order to go beyond Cuba's borders and intervene in Latin America, he confronted the United States government. . . .

We are aware that measures have been taken [against the regime]. Castro has received plenty of advice of late. His regime knows well that so long as he keeps on the present course he will not have any credibility with those countries that do respect human rights. Having this in mind, then, what we wish is for additional measures to be taken. But not merely the type of moral measures of warning, for example: "We denounce you because you violate human rights systematically." Sanctions must be imposed similar to the ones applied to other governments that systematically violated human rights, such as South Africa's which had a system that offended human dignity. It is simply not enough to condemn and denounce over and over if sanctions are not imposed with the aim of having the dictator change, or else have him realize that his end is at hand and that he must go. That is all. Leaving, giving up power, is the only thing that he and his group could do in order to save the country's situation so that it does not continue to slide into chaos and we can therefore avert a terrible bloodbath.

CLINTON, CASTRO AND GUANTANAMERA

While ballots are still being counted in Mexico, and in L.A., and the least details of the Simpson case are the stuff of every talk show,

Cuba is undergoing a civil hemorrhage to which Washington is responding with a reactive policy, typical of its attitude toward Latin America in general. As of this writing (August 28th) almost twelve thousand *balseros* had already arrived at the Guantanamo Naval Base. The figure includes only those who have been picked up by the U.S. Coast Guard for the previous ten days, not the other several thousand who since mid-June have taken to the sea seeking political asylum in the U.S. under the Cuban Adjustment Act.* Neither does it include those who, under the absurd regulations that govern the present situation, are able to escape the Coast Guard's watch and land on one of the Florida keys before being booked. The hemorrhage threatens to last indefinitely, even while talks between the U.S. and Cuban governments are held ("but only low-level," added State Department spokesmen) on the subject of their migration agreement. Around those talks rages another, wider debate, however, on the subject of the lifting of the U.S. embargo against the Castro regime and how best to persuade Castro to open to democratic reform.

Once Castro began to allow, and even encourage, the exodus — Miami exiles began calling it the "slow-motion Mariel" — the Administration's response proved swift and harsh. Not only did it order every *balsero* picked up and ferried to Guantánamo for further processing to a third country, it also closed down all charter flights between Miami and Havana and stopped dollar remittances to relatives on the island. The former was a reaction to Florida Governor Lawton Chiles's cry for help before the coming refugee crisis; the latter the result of the pressures exerted upon President Clinton by the Cuban-American lobby, which used the crisis to press one of its oldest and most cherished goals: to cut the flow of dollars to the regime from the very exile community it represents. The cut, presently estimated at 500 million dollars annually, deals a hard strategic blow to Havana. And yet, the same success could not be claimed for Clinton's *guantanamera* policy.

The U.S. government has not figured out that the rafters aren't just interested in getting to the United States. They want out of

---

*On May 3, 1995, the Clinton administration announced a major overhaul of U.S.-Cuban refugee policy. There are still thirty-thousand rafters housed in Guántanamo Naval Base, among them five thousand children under the age of twelve.

Cuba. They are not being held back by "the lack of credibility of Clinton's foreign policy," which is how one *New York Times* columnist put it: they're leaving because they're hungry, afraid, and desperate. For the past thirty years Cubans have been defecting all over: Gander and San Juan, Stockholm, Madrid, and even Moscow. And many of them choose to stay put. That is why the Guántanamo ferry was not able, nor will it be able if the same conditions were to recur, to put a halt to the wave of refugees, or to the unwitting responsibility of the U.S. government before it.

That is why talks between the two governments will attempt to agree on something substantial: if Castro will once again guard the Cuban coastline, Clinton will allow more Cubans to enter the U.S. legally, that is, through visas granted at the U.S. Interests Section in Havana, up to the twenty-thousand per year quota. Neither Havana nor Washington can hide from the fact, however, that even as they agree on this policy it can only be a short-term measure with unsatisfying results. While Washington and the Cuban-American community want Castro to open up in a way that the Cuban leader does not favor, Havana on the other hand demands an economic flexibility that would assure the regime's survival.

Some political analysts, among them Bernard Aronson and Gillian Gunn, assure us that unless there is a previous opening of the economic front (i.e., if the embargo is lifted), there won't be any political concessions on Castro's part. The reason is simple, they say: the regime wants to take credit for whatever prosperity there is after the embargo is lifted, and thus assure for itself a victory at the polls within a new democratic framework. The same analysts don't seem to have ever heard, however, that beggars can't be choosers. And in this case everyone knows that the beggar's name is Fidel Castro. Neither do they question—and here lies the morally repugnant aspect of their point—whether such a premise goes against the most fundamental rules of the democratic game—nobody is given a head start and it is up to the people to decide who is best able to lead them. Why not demand for Cuba the same democratic rules that Aronson and Gunn would demand for free elections in the U.S. or Britain?

Which people are we talking about, incidentally? Who defines the collective? I would say that it's made up not only of those who live in the island and have chosen to stay, but also all exiles who wish to return and live there. Whatever agreement the U.S. and Cuban governments reach eventually, and they should, it must perforce include the legitimate interests of the Cuban exile community, residing both in the U.S. and abroad. The exile community counts among its members as many prominent political leaders as reside today inside Cuba, mostly within the numerous but virtually clandestine human rights organizations. And while that community ought certainly not to occupy a preponderant place in political discussion, neither should it be excluded in order to satisfy the desired advantages of the regime.

The issue of democratization ought to be discussed as a priority, then, and it also ought to be conditioned upon the decriminalization of all political activity outside of the Cuban Communist Party. Such a premise would include, of course, all peaceful political activity on the part of Cuban exile groups. And given that the majority of those groups operate within the United States, the premise ought to be specifically conditioned on the renewal of dollar remittances to Cuba. If the Castro regime sees fit to recognize the importance of what it calls "the Cuban community abroad" by cashing in its commissions on dollar remittances, then it ought similarly to recognize that community's right to participate in its public life. And Cuban exiles ought to do no less by demanding it.

The call to a dialogue with Castro only makes sense if the agenda includes those issues that the regime does *not* wish to discuss: the end of Castroism, free and internationally supervised elections, human rights, the guarantee of so-called formal freedoms (free expression, press and market forces), as well as the recognition of the legitimate role of the exile community in Cuba's political future. My friend Jorge Domínguez, arguably the world's leading expert on Cuba, remarks that the embargo ought not to be an altar but a tool for change. I would add, however, that change ought to be moral and political and not just economic. It should demand guarantees for public life, including the right of Cubans to commerce among citizens, — not simply an extension of credits, a version of foreign aid, to a regime that is now trying to avoid total bankruptcy. The latter only happens to be the case because the so-called embargo is a convenient theme for Castro — never before, while he enjoyed billions in subsidies from the Soviets was it an issue — and it has became an urgent topic ever since the stampede caused by the senseless decision to dollarize the Cuban economy began in earnest.

The key word for the lifting of the embargo is *negotiation*. It should not be lifted simply because that is what Castro happens to wish. If it is *not* negotiated, not only will there be no political change in Cuba but the refugee problem that worries the administration so much will not cease and the human and economic cost will increase ceaselessly.

TEMMA EHRENFELD

HAROLD THE HIGH LAMA

It began on a nice morning, an ideal morning. No delay on the
subway, no unwashed armpits under his nose. Between bites of his
sesame bagel and swallows of coffee (two packets of sweetener),
Harold watered his pink and red impatiens. Sunshine poured over
the rooftops onto a quiet telephone.

Normally he had to satisfy himself with the radio and a glance at
the *Times* before his first, most irritating job of the morning: scan-
ning and correcting Earl's entries from the previous day. Earl would
saunter in at ten-thirty or so, and while Earl was aware of his
cleanups, relied upon them, in fact, Harold felt a public display
would disturb the pride of both parties. Only on Earl's day off (or if
he'd been especially lazy the day before and didn't have much product requiring review) could Harold indulge in a full hour with his
coffee and papers before the electronic chirping began, the perpet-
ual call of the unselfreliant world.

At 10:00 the week's issue arrived, bearing a not-bad cover. Harold
with a seasoned hand turned snappily to the masthead. Ah. The
rumored ascent of the librarians had been pleasing him for months;
just the concept of his old friends acknowledged, at last, aroused a
family glow. Three of the current staff of six he'd known since his
arrival the summer after community college, back when they'd sat
together at the long clipping desk—nobody's scalp in sight, Harold's
glossy brown mane down to his ass. Bunch of freaks making a buck
off the media-man.

Native talent had won Harold promotion to the Index behind
Earl, where he placidly watched as the others plowed through
library-science school. While they sat in night class, he watched
movies with his then-wife and cats. They became librarians; he
made almost as much by staying himself.

Assistant editor: Jerry, Mary, Patrick. Senior editorial assistant: Earl, Chris. Editorial assistant: Lorraine, Judith.

Earl?

I'll kill him.

Harold stared at the printed column, his glow reduced to a small hot spot center-chest, where the knife came to quivering rest.

Chris got his degree two years later than Patrick. So Chris below Patrick could have been anticipated. Lorraine and Judith didn't have the years.

Chirp. First ring of the day, evenly spaced. Chirp. A member of the public seeking information: insider rings came in pairs.

Who would have guessed that Earl, as chief of the Index department — chief of Harold, that was, by virtue of a year's seniority — would show up in the printed ranks? Paperless Earl, dummy to Harold's ventriloquist.

Chirp.

I'll kill him.

Chirp.

"Index, Harold speaking."

The woman on the other end wanted to know the date of the cover story on the strongest breed of ox, the Xhangsu ox.

"We've done no such story." He knew the covers by heart.

"I find that hard to believe."

"We've done no such story." For repetition he used his best genial but firm tone. Although Harold considered kooks the pro-bono part of his job, he was in no mood. "But thank you for calling. Excuse me, I have another call. . . ." He put her on hold. "Index, Harold speaking."

This woman's son had a report to do. She'd like the dates of all articles on computers in the last six months or so.

"Computers? Computers are one of the major topics of our time. We have two new sections entirely devoted to computers. Can you be more specific?"

That was the assignment.

"You do your son no service doing his work for him. I'm sure he was given this assignment to learn how to use a library. What I would suggest that your son do is go to the public library and check the *Reader's Guide to Periodical Literature* in the periodicals section. Have him look under computers. He'll find all the articles that we and other publications have done on the subject."

"*The Reader's Guide*. . . . Oh of course you're right. You're absolutely right. You know how it is with children. . . ."

"Of course I do."

Harold always scolded the mothers, in a pleasant enough fashion such that they responded in a chastened manner and rushed off not angry but abashed. This one fled.

The Xhangsu ox button had remained lit. "Hello?"

"I'm holding. For the date of the cover story on the Xhangsu ox?"

"We've done no such story."

"Did you check? I know there's a cover story. On the cover. I don't believe you've even looked for it."

"If you insist . . ." He put her on hold again and started up a game of solitaire on the screen. He'd turned over twenty-two cards and moved three aces up, a good sixty seconds, when he looked back at his telephone. Her square light had gone dark.

Some are born to sweet delight. Some are born to endless night.

Harold liked tangibles, CDs, good coffee, a gold watch the year his mutual fund earned twenty-two. He couldn't remember the last time he'd wanted anything he couldn't buy.

Harold wanted his name on the masthead.

That was it: his name in the tiny column, his name among all the others he knew by heart because he had typed their names and chronicled their articles for twenty years. Reporters, writers, editors: information shovels who took pride in forgetting the subject of the day's panic once their heads hit their pillows. Only Harold remembered. Harold memorized the magazine, which few of them even read: its glossy cover constituted a kind of coffin to them; from a staff point of view, typeface in print might as well have been dead.

Cover worked for Cover, Business for Business. Only Harold worked for the magazine itself. Harold, keeper of the index, memory of a nation without memory: If any name should have been on the masthead, it should have been his.

Harold had a quote and citation for every occasion. Earl's memory had creative revisionist force. Harold had front of the book, Earl back, front being twice the job. Earl liked to sit at Harold's desk in his absence, strewing empty styrofoam cups and doodles on Harold's clean pad. Earl liked to spread out. He forgot to index subjects that failed to interest him, or offended him, like, say, anything on punk or jazz (he favored opera), or the America's Cup (hated sports).

Only Harold, master of the tricks of Earl's digital dyslexia, knew to tell the computer to search for Brynat instead of Bryant.

"Good morning," Earl trumpeted, sliding in with breakfast in tow. "I'm a little late." He remarked upon it daily. "Would you believe I got stopped by a policeman. On the corner of 42nd. Would you believe he asked for I.D. I told him this is not East Germany, I am not required to carry I.D. I'm a bicyclist, I'm not required to carry a license. He asked for my name and I told him Jack Jykes."

"What were you doing?"

"I was turning onto 42nd with the light. A very noisy fat woman who did not have the right of way was shouting at me when the policeman came up out of nowhere. Can you believe the nerve of that cop? Taking me for a messenger boy?"

Earl, one knew, did not have the right of way. Nor would he care to hear Harold's opinion of lawless selfish bicyclists, who were above even taxidrivers in his personal hates. Earl had seated himself at his desk, in the crotch of an L, the short side of which touched Harold's L, when Harold leaned over and handed him the issue open at the masthead. "I had a surprise this morning."

Earl quickly found his name. "How nice!" said Earl, and dropped the magazine on Harold's half.

Harold mentally picked up the typewriter and hurled it at his head. "I'm not on it."

"You're not on it?" Earl uncapped his coffee. He looked out his window. Earl assiduously avoided eye contact. "That's a disgrace. It's an insult to the Index. You ought to speak up." Earl slurped. "Jack Jykes. I'd like to see Jack Jykes on the masthead as senior editorial assistant."

Chirp chirp. An inside call. Earl tilted his coffee again to his mouth. Chirp chirp.

It was understood that if Earl was eating, or occupied on the other line with a friend, calls went unanswered. Unless Harold picked up, which Harold unfailingly did.

"Index, Harold speaking."

Up, down, over, to the computer, rifling his index cards, reaching for his bound volumes, scolding, reassuring. Harold served. Service warmed him like a microwave, from the core out. All he asked was recognition; all he asked was justice. He felt better when Earl vanished to the gym.

"Index. Harold speaking."

"Hello Harold Speaking. This is Eva with an R in front." Reva called ritually at 3:30, if they hadn't had lunch, surfacing with Harold for gulps of air before re-ramming her mole nose into the dirt of personal finance. "I have called 40 people since lunch. I have spelled my name 40 times and given my phone number 40 times, and explained that it's a palindrome, same backwards and forwards, 465-4564. If anyone calls me back now, they can get the machine, I'm not talking."

"It's only Monday."

"Joan's going to the Galapagos Wednesday. We're closing early."

"I just got a call from Letters looking for the story on the top grossing summer movies last year. It had a statistical box, a photo, and text, and not a one of them was indexed. Earl forgot. I had to look through all of July and August by hand."

From the party her first week on the job, Reva had appreciated that Harold's art lay in giving. Harold gave year-round. He'd fetched her a drink and a plate with two crackers spread neatly with paté (the crackers, both for her, she hadn't asked for), and guided her about the room from one higher-up to another, standing silent by her side as she tried to impress. All this just being nice; she'd dropped her new boyfriend's name into the conversation as soon as one could and be polite.

Harold, sparkle in a black rock. Her last company had been full of shits, but sociable shits, socializing up. What you did here was fossilize in the rock. Reva could feel time pressing her into tracings, simultaneously abstract and concrete, of the girl they hired. Reva-senior-editorial-assistant, neither dead nor alive. Defined.

Harold lived. He'd amused Reva no end with tales of Earl's incompetence, keeping them light, betraying no hurt. The rather shocking tales of the ex-wife's selfishness he made amusing, too.

"I guess you couldn't just leave a note on his desk and let him do it?"

"Did you see the masthead?"

"No."

"Get it."

Reva put him on hold. Harold turned over three cards. "I got it." Reva spread the magazine open at her cubicle and examined the column of print. She found her name first. Reva Erdman. Right after Earl Darling.

"Earl's a senior editorial assistant?" Masthead titles bore no relationship to what one did.

"Isn't that nice?"

She resented it, not that she cared. They'd put the library in: Jerry, Mary, Patrick. Chris. Lorraine, Judith. "I don't see you."

"I'm not on," said Harold, and they both suffered as his voice broke. "He's on and I'm not. I knew I wouldn't be. I didn't know he'd be."

Poor Harold. He deserved better. Indexer and reporter together heard the thin unconvincing tone in her voice as she murmured, "You know what this place is like. It's not as if he's going to get more money or more respect, anything you'd really want."

"I want to be on the masthead."

What was a senior editorial assistant supposed to say? Harold gave her ten seconds and couldn't bear any more. "Do me a favor. Change the subject."

"Get any kooks today?"

"A woman who insisted we'd done a cover on the Xhangsu ox."

"The what?"

"A Chinese ox."

"What made her think there'd be a story?"

"Not a story. A cover. She says it's the strongest breed of ox. I say, we've done no such story." Harold mimicked, "I find that hard to believe."

Reva's giggle! Reva at least appreciated him. "I call this the grape juice phenomenon. I had a woman who swore we'd done a cover on the new grape juice. There was a new way of making concentrate."

"I guess everybody thinks what they think is important is important." Poor Harold. "Are you going to complain?"

Harold had never once complained to a superior about any aspect of his job. His time had come.

Harold whined to the head of the library, plump Ed; Ed asked him for a memo. The memo, one sheet single-spaced, copy-edited by the former chief of the copy desk long since retired (she still came by for Harold's help in settling dinner-party arguments) lay from January to April in a pile on Ed's desk.

Harold spoke to several of the librarians discreetly and privately about his own effort. Each said the masthead made no difference, off it or on. Now a bonus, a raise, *that* would be nice. Harold was sure they were all lying.

Easy for them to say, their noses weren't pressed against the window. Easy for them to say, they didn't slog beside the luckiest, happiest, most self-centered man on God's earth. Earl planned to die at the peak of his credit limit. He scoffed at Harold's self-disciplined contributions to the corporate savings plan, oblivious to the needs of a college-bound son, whom Earl had known from babyhood, and never asked after.

Harold couldn't not overhear the intrigue, cultural opinions and mourning of Earl's adolescent whirl of romance and gang gatherings, hardly sobered in his case by the steady toll of the plague. Earl's luck had held; he tested clean. Earl didn't use his vacation days to drop in on the hospital patients and funerals; he just took the day off, leaving Harold alone to the phones, with nary a thank you.

How could one tattle? How could one complain, it doesn't take an eight-hour day to visit a hospital patient?

When Harold remarked darkly on the impotence of his memo, Earl airily waved. "It's just the masthead," he said.

The keeper of the index understood the exact significance of the masthead. History buff and loyalist, he read hefty biographies and hung on the wall his collection of presidential plaques. No slab of bronze, silver or gold, would ever bear Harold's profile; no one would care to study his turning points. But at least he knew enough to appreciate the vastness of time and the company of the greats.

Earl saw only his own noble face. That Earl and not he should be granted this small immortality, that was unjust.

Harold's tales of Earl's mishaps acquired a certain edge. Reva, plastic fork in midair, would stare at him, her round hazel eyes concerned.

"You know what?" she said. "I was watching *Lost Horizon* on TV the other night, the late late show, and I thought, out of everybody I know who would I pick to be the boss of paradise? Someone has to be in charge. Who's loving and fair and not into himself? Harold. You could be the High Lama."

Reva's suede skirt clung to her round belly, as she sat on the park bench; her short muscley legs balanced her like the cabriole legs of the night table his ex wouldn't give up. A carrot sliver from her takeout salad had come to rest in the crack where her black angora fuzzed over her sweetly girlish breasts. Harold had to struggle not to kiss her.

It was the first decent day of March, bright and warm at 65, the end of a bad winter that had kept them eating in the subsidized rinkydink cafeteria, their voices raised automatically to drown the garbage compactor's continual wheeze.

Reva had been analyzing character, specifically her boyfriend's, in biz school in Cambridge. He had taken a disturbing turn, she felt; he seemed limited and selfish.

"You're a good person, you're *good*. That's the important thing," said Reva, her eyes moist.

Harold sprung to action as if he'd seen a toddler stumbling over a curb. "What? What is it?"

"Just give me a minute."

"Tell me."

"You must be so sick of this."

"Another phone call."

"This weekend is the function I had to buy that dress for. I don't want to go. I don't want to."

"Tell him."

"He's counting on me. I said I would, I went last year. I was so miserable. He was working all day and then in the evening we had to be with these boring pretentious people. I hated them. I absolutely hated them and we had this big fight that night. He was defending them. He said I humiliated him."

"You humiliated him?"

"This creepy professor was grilling me about variable universal life insurance, there's this totally abusive tax scheme he was into, and I told him I thought Congress was going to get rid of it and I hoped they would. The country can't afford it."

"You did." Reva, Reva, defending the public good.

"Steven said I'd insulted him."

"You're not allowed to have politics?"

"Not when he's busy social-climbing. He's so insecure. It's understandable, he's always working. He's worked so hard." Reva's salad teetered on her lap; Harold reached out to steady it. "There's the train ticket and that dress wasn't cheap. It's a lot of money so I can be miserable."

"You could call in sick?"

"I wish."

The kid—like policemen, they got younger every year—solved a lot of problems for Reva, even Harold could see that. When she'd been paying for lunch a few weeks ago he'd noticed a photo in her wallet, and against his better judgment asked if he could look. A weak chin, but blond, and a Jewish high-holiday temple-goer too, a sort of faux *shaygut*. Reva even when she starved herself didn't lose her belly, her hair had a frizzy temperament, and she was already 32. Reva in the course of her job couldn't help trying to calculate what she'd need to save to retire at 65 at her present middle-middle class standard of living assuming she lived to 90; she also knew the cost of nannies.

The relationship has been mutually profitable, thought Harold, bitterness bursting in him as if from a pimple on his heart. A phrase from his memo to Ed. The memo had entered his lexicon of quotes.

Over Reva's dark head, Harold saw the Yankee cap of his regular dealer, the one whose bags seemed infinitesimally plumper.

"I'll be back in a minute," said Harold, and within seconds had his dime bag. *Mutually profitable.* He returned to find the carrot sliver gone and Reva running her finger through the French dressing on the side of her plastic takeout box. She looked up, finger in her mouth, swiftly guiltily removed. "I'm *hungry*."

"Would you like me to slug him for you, Reva?" She'd confessed that he dropped hints about her weight.

"Steven?" Reva's eyes shone dangerously again. "Oh, the diet's for me. I guess. I can't remember now. Do you think I'm so weepy because I'm not eating enough? Low blood sugar? I think that's it."

"We've got fifteen minutes. If we go now, you can get some more salad."

Reva folded her box shut, held it with one hand, and slung her bag over her shoulder with the other. "You really think the stuff's okay in the park? What if it's laced with rat poison? Could you tell?"

"It's okay."

"Harold, could you do me a huge favor? I wouldn't ask, except . . . remember the roaches all over my kitchen, it's a horror movie turning on the light at night. I called the exterminator this morning, they can only come Thursday next week, but they won't tell me what time. I can't get out of work, anyway." Thursdays, Harold worked from 4:00 to midnight.

"You want me to be there?"

"What do you think? Should I let him come in with nobody there?"

"I wouldn't. I'll do it."

Actually, he'd like being in her apartment, like the feel of her in the beige paisley sofa, the china with flowered rims, little rocks and seashells on the top of the toilet. He liked everything but the bare walls; Reva wanted oils, not prints, and oils she couldn't afford. He liked that, too, didn't he, her stubborn incompleteness, her eye up. The eye that turned a dried-out artichoke into art.

He had been there only once, after a movie, when he came up for the bathroom and a little domesticity before the hell ahead: waiting for an F on a Sunday night. Another look would be nice.

Late lonely nights, Harold cherished secret hopes that one day she'd get foolish and see Harold. Not that he didn't see her conflict. Romantic he might be, not blind, his crush a cloud edged in conclusive dark violet.

Piano notes floated like holograms in the center of his Kew Gardens efficiency as Harold the High Lama up in smoke lay on his bed under his cabinet of bronze medals. Through the holograms he faced a portrait-sized celluloid pin of Eisenhower's moon face and boyish smile. Ike smiling young lawns and barbecues Harold, son of tenements, had yet to see, but recalled; Harold knew his TV history, knew his magazine covers. Memory of an aphasic nation, at home Jeopardy king.

Ike knew he deserved a place on the masthead. Ike knew each man had his role, even Democrats. In Ike-land, a good soldier got the girl.

If he won the lottery? Swept Jeopardy? Made the masthead?

Harold, a long sufferer of subway armpits (middleaged men from certain neighborhoods in Queens rarely washed their clothing), positioned his chair and his nose such that he could smell Reva's armpits when she stood beside him at his desk—it seemed to him now, in his pleasant confusion, that her odor hung in the air. Could it be that Reva smelled like the blessing of grass?

My position in the Library Index Department requires that I provide important editorial assistance. I provide this assistance with a high degree of skill and accuracy that is second to none in the department.

Many editors, writers and researchers have come to rely on my personal assistance in retrieving articles from sixty-one years of publication, as well as facts and details from our articles and other sources.

I am the only library staffer who works late Thursday and Friday nights and Saturdays assisting editors, writers and researchers in closing the week's issue whose name does not appear on the masthead.

My Index Department co-worker, whose job and duties are identical to my own, appears on the masthead as Senior Editorial Assistant. I carry more than my share of the duties and responsibilities for running the Index operation.

I have been with the magazine for twenty years. The relationship has been mutually profitable.

I would be very proud to be publically associated with this publication by having my name appear on the masthead, and I believe the reasons I have cited render this a justifiable request.

Thank you for your attention to this matter.

Decisions such as these were made in January, Ed told him on a rainy afternoon in April — April 4, 1993, to be precise. Harold did not point out that the memo had sat on Ed's desk for three weeks in January.

February 19, 1994, cold, grey and windy, he called Harold into his corner office. "They" had said No. He was sorry.

"They" surely being the man at the top, the last male Meredith in New York. Editor-in-chief Meredith Barnum, a man with the height and ruddy complexion and stick up the posterior gait of a South African magnate, would be unlikely to delegate decisions regarding the masthead.

Ed explained that getting Harold on meant also listing two others with his title, library assistant; three more names they couldn't do.

Harold thanked him for his efforts on his behalf. He doubted that Ed had in fact made efforts on his behalf, but he was a strong believer in not pissing in a well from which he might have to drink.

Rage like a fireplace burned his backside while he presented his cool face to the staffers who called for his help that night. His third consecutive Friday night, Earl having begged off to see Damian star at the ballet. Rage burst into flame at midnight as he waited for the elevator home.

Meredith alone, from 25. No eye contact, never eye contact. The man nodded back, this being America. In America you nodded, even if you didn't speak to the likes of Harold.

May you burn in hell.

Meredith visibly uncomfortable at the proximity of Harold in the descending box not because he felt a curse or even knew who Harold was; Meredith uncomfortable the way Harold was uncomfortable seizing his crisp twenties from the ATM, alone in *that* bright box but for the pungent human heap on the floor, at his feet, with bottle or cup.

Cold slugged Harold in the eyes as he emerged from the revolving door into the night, one partition behind Meredith. He'd rather wait inside. . . . But Meredith stood regal, Burberry scarf cascading cravat-style from his chin. Harold, by union agreement, was entitled to a car after nine o'clock, and after ten minutes on hold with Neil Diamond croaking about immigrants "all coming to America" in his ear — Harold saw Mike Dukakis striding to the podium — he'd been promised #236 in eight minutes. The elevator had used up at least five.

Yes! #236 drove up. Harold grabbed it. Meredith stood impassive, accepting his fate.

Harold lost sleep. The insistent noise of memo language typing itself on his brain woke him in the early hours. A black and gray column magnified before his eyes: hallucinating, or a dream? Earl Darling Reva Erdman.

Never one to hide his fancy associations, he had without documentation impressed whomever there was to impress. One of the doormen, an intellectual type who had a tragedy of some kind under his belt, pontificated at Harold about distortions in coverage. A fourteen-year-old nephew called begging Harold to get him into a sold-out concert. Clearly these two hadn't checked the fine print of the masthead.

Alone in his office, Reva put her hand to his forehead, checking for fever.

"Earl did it again. It took me an hour to find what they wanted."

"I don't know why you keep covering for him."

"It isn't me, it isn't him, it's the Index. I'm covering my ass."

"No you're not. It's always back of the book you can't find. That's his ass. You're just public spirited. You think his ass is your ass."

"One ass with two cheeks."

"Why don't you just say you'll leave a note for the person respon-sible. Leave it on his desk."

"Have you seen his desk?"

"Tape them to the computer screen."

"I can't."

"You can."

"I can't stand by while the house burns down."

"Let it burn."

"Why? Why should I?"

"You don't get rewarded for eating shit. Maybe if you didn't clean up after him you'd be more appreciated. He might even get fired."

"Is that what I do? Eat shit?"

A long pause. "I'm sorry. I'm a dybbuk talking, I should have my mouth washed out. You're being good and I'm making you feel bad about it."

Another memo, this time explaining why he should be considered separately from the other library assistants. Only Harold dealt with the public; only Harold worked round the clock election nights; only Harold. . . .

He took the imperious step of sneaking into Ed's office during lunch and leaving memo two on his chair. That way, he'd have to read it before settling down to an afternoon's wheeling and dealing. Ed rarely emerged from his office, but he did have to pass through the library to get to the elevators, and he liked to stop over some-body's desk just long enough to force the targeted employee to put a caller on hold.

"Just watching you work," he'd say, with a delighted grin. Or "Only 300 shopping days to Christmas!," a joke that appeared peri-odically, whenever Ed got a yen to play with his calculator. Cast as Santa by a nursery school teacher years before, Ed still showed up annually (his children adolescent now — he'd liked them better lit-tle). A white beard, pregnant middle and bright neckties contrib-uted to his year-round air of presiding over a tribe of elves, pre-sumed happy by association with his substantial jolly self. Should an elf alarm him with discontent, Ed went as peevish as a man whose beard has been yanked painfully off, cover blown.

Harold from the Index area heard Ed's high voice in the main open space of the library, and a few minutes later, the phone chirped an insider.

"Index, Harold speaking."

Ed brisk, pained, requesting his presence in his office.

"What is going on, Harold," said Ed, as Harold entered. Ed waved conspiratorially at the door, which Harold closed. "I thought you understood the situation."

"I do understand. I mean to address the specific concern you expressed to me, that the category of library assistant doesn't belong on the masthead as a group. I believe my case should be considered separately."

"You know I tried."

"I appreciate that."

"I'd like to pass this on," said Ed, meaning he wouldn't at all like to.

Harold, as he spoke, found the correct modulation of urgency and gravity. "I would be very proud to be publically associated with this magazine. I believe that with further consideration the company will realize that it would do well to encourage that sentiment in its employees. Loyalty is not to be sniffed at."

"Your loyalty is certainly appreciated."

Harold had not been invited to sit. He sat. He looked at Ed. Ed's eyes widened.

"This isn't like you."

"It's become important to me."

"Tilting at windmills? I don't get it, Harold."

"I don't mean to sound like a jealous sibling, but there are only two of us and I do more than my share in running the Index operation."

Ed stared. "You've had your twentieth anniversary, haven't you?"

"Almost two years ago. March 15, 1992."

"It's possible that could set you apart. That could be a point. The others don't have twenty years."

"Twenty-two. I could address the memo to the appropriate parties on my own behalf."

"Oh, I wouldn't do that!" said Ed, meaning Harold would be eaten alive in the dangerous waters upstairs. "I can't promise anything. I have to say I'd be surprised. Asking for a reversal of an earlier decision, that doesn't go down well." Ed looked meaningfully at Harold, who nodded; he knew better than to speak. "Twenty-two years. That's a point. Who knows, I've been surprised before."

"Index, Harold speaking."

A woman who wanted to know everything they'd done on South Africa, and Mandela, and de Klerk, and apartheid.

"That's quite a list. Can you be more specific?"

She couldn't. Her boss's child had a report.

"Not even your child." He couldn't scold the women who called for bosses. Two of his most frequent regulars called for the children of bosses in the back copies and circulation departments.

Yeah, what a creep. But he's a boss. She had to do it, the woman explained. Would you believe the kid is a freshman in college? Harold believed it.

Chirp. "Index, Harold speaking."

A mother concerned about her daughter's teacher, who had put forth a theory explaining how rocks reproduce.

"First of all you've reached the Index, where you can find the dates that articles have appeared in this magazine. I'm afraid we're not offering a general research service."

"He's wrong, isn't he? Doesn't that sound funny to you?"

"Well, we've done no such story on the reproduction of rocks."

"You're highly respected. If I can say you say what he's teaching is false I could enclose it with my letter to the principal. Is there anything. . .under geology, you think? I need proof."

"We've done no such story on the reproduction of rocks or the lack thereof," said Harold. "What exactly did he say?"

"He has a theory. I don't know the details. My daughter said he said rocks reproduce."

"Possibly by being smashed into pieces, he's calling that reproduction?"

"I can't tell you any more, what can I say?"

"You'll never be able to prove that rocks don't reproduce. People should be required to prove that rocks do reproduce."

"They won't listen to me. I don't know about rocks."

"What I suggest is you put in your letter that you're extremely concerned and you'd like to see him prove that rocks do reproduce. Put him on the defensive. Okay? Good luck with it now."

Harold had personally experienced the problem this mother faced: the difficulty of proving a negative. Editors had a way of being certain of the existence of nonexistent articles, and if Harold couldn't locate the phantom from the details given, Harold would be told via the secretary to try again. Stretch dates and topics like rubber bands, and he'd give the secretary everything but what she wanted, irritating all concerned. What bothered Harold was the impossibility of pleasing, and the impossibility of removing from himself the onus of failure. Any editor who so chose could presume Harold wrong unless he went back and looked at each and every issue himself.

The success of memo two could well rest on what happened should Meredith call with a request. If the request had to do with his own indexing, he had confidence. His answer might disappoint Meredith but at least it would be correct. The problem would arise if Meredith called and asked for an article in Earl's area. If Earl had screwed up, and if Harold hadn't caught him, Harold might lose his chance at immortality.

Reva knew Steven needed to lean on her when he had all those job interviews and exams coming up, that he'd have no attention to spare. It wouldn't always be this bad, or maybe it would, but Reva by habit, if nothing else, persisted. In preparation for their regular Sunday night call, she tended to ignore the helpful offer on her takeout menu of vegetables prepared without oil, salt, or MSG, and order the fat and sugar instead. Self-medication, she calmly observed, fat to calm you, sugar for cheer. Harold performed the same functions for her more healthily at work.

Reva on a diet again did a new thing: she called Harold at home. Harold in Queens, with his own area code, had just as long a number as Steve's up in Boston. Funny how the telephone made you feel close to people who weren't close, and far from people who weren't far.

"Hello."

"Hi."

"Well, hello."

"What were you doing?"

"Just hanging around."

"No, tell me."

"I really wasn't doing anything."

"You can't do nothing."

"I can too."

"C'mon. Were you thinking?"

"Actually no."

"Looking out the window?"

"Maybe I don't want to tell you."

"Oh."

"What were you doing?"

"Thinking."

"Of course."

He sounded so far away, so in his own private place. Reva imagined a square of light in a highrise. The thought comforted her, and it was better that she hadn't actually seen Harold's home. She would instantly begin thinking of ways to change it, Harold would see revision in her eyes and be insulted.

"Kids don't know how lucky they are." Reva settled into her pillows for a chat. "Being an adult is terrible. You're always either bored or anxious." Of course it could be that those were simply her only options available in the company of Steven, coloring her outlook, the way men did. It was true, though: what she wanted she'd already had as a child, and lost: comfort, security and fresh, justified optimism each summer, each fall. Each fall new things to learn, a new class. Out by three o'clock.

"I know what will cheer you up."

"What?"

"You have to take the F train. I've got movies. I've got all the best movies ever made."

"Now?"

"Are you busy Saturday?"

"I'm going to Boston, probably, unless he's too busy."

"You don't sound happy about it," said Harold, gently; he had not lost patience.

And so Reva talked about Steven, she couldn't stop once she'd started and she felt better telling him, although she felt guilty for a little bit after she hung up, only a little bit because Harold always had patience.

Harold gleamed fresh and white and invitingly open, like a teacup, shaped to be used.

She would have asked him if he'd heard about the masthead, except he'd told her not to; he'd tell her when he heard. She liked to ask, to float the balloon and gaze up—his name in the printed column. With people you loved you wanted to see their baby pictures, you imagined their futures, you talked in three tenses. Harold made things uncomfortably flat.

Private past was the marriage — not to linger on. The same job for twenty years, and then another twenty — Reva couldn't bear to think what that meant.

Reva herself was *spinning her wheels, stuck, in a rut*; Steven had pointed it out. He said when he had a chance after school, he'd sit down with her and they'd make a map of how she would get to where she wanted to be by thirty-five. Reva had been touched, grateful for his promise to lend his personality to jumpstart hers (and somewhere in there they'd get to discuss the kids), but still, a perverse inertia in her argued *I'm not a car. One car in the family is enough.*

He would insist on two cars. He'd want her to stay stimulating; he liked to tell his friends she worked for the magazine they read on planes.

Reva that night heard Steven's body in his rushed emphatic voice. She heard the blood that bulged the lightning-flash vein in his forehead whenever he lay sideways on her bed, and she said good night as quickly as she could. He'd aroused her in a yucky nervous way that couldn't be satisfied; afterwards, you always felt worse. Reva broke down and found the peanut butter hidden on the top shelf, stuck her finger in and out, sucked.

Rumors of cutbacks circulated in the library, a vague forecast a day, like newspaper horoscopes, each class of worker with its own fate. A team from Steven's managment consulting firm — he'd been snapped up after graduation, begun work in June — had been called in to evaluate all support-service functions. Nobody knew what the firm had recommended be done.

Of course, it made no difference what some evaluating team said, and everybody knew that, too. Decisions would be made at the top, by at-the-top reasoning. Evaluating teams were just the excuse.

Still, Reva asked Steven if he could try to see what had been said. They fought. Steven couldn't believe she'd even asked. He'd never jeopardize the company's trust. Did she care so little about his future?

Reva, schooled by hours at the gym trying to treadmill away her genetically-coded belly, knew when she was pressing against irrelevant resistance. She knew instantly what would be used and what not when her assignments came in, the unneeded information always the bigger challenge. Still, she treaded, she reported, and she fought — on a Friday night, even though Steven had to be in the office the rest of the weekend.

Ed forgot to flush, Harold noted, on following him into the one-stall handicapped bathroom. Nerves. Ed had been seen on the telephone with panic bright in his eyes.

His secretary, shaking her head sadly, spoke of nasty E-mail. Clippers, filers beware. The union that made it difficult to fire Earl alone couldn't prevent the firing of many at once. Poor kids in the back would suffer. The quickest pair of scissors, the brightest tattoo on a bicep, cigarettes smoked or given up, wouldn't save them now.

Harold couldn't sleep. There had been no response to his second memo; he revenged himself in dreams. Earl and his bicycle crashing to the ground, sirens screaming; Earl mansize in a diaper, screaming; Earl as emaciated marionette, Harold yanking Earl's strings, Earl screaming.

If the Index were to be cut, leaving one, Earl normally would be the one, Earl having seniority. Harold sleepless reasoned that Ed would be insecure with Earl to rely on. Ed would have to save Harold.

One day a memo appeared on his desk. The clippers and filers, like roaches, must move to other pipes. The magazine would be relying on computer services instead.

Harold inquired. Three out of twelve had been offered slots in circulation, an hour and a half away by bus in Clear Streams, New Jersey. Clear Streams, however, had been bought by another outfit, nonunionized, that made you pay for most of your health insurance. Part-timers didn't get insured at all. In the two weeks after the announcement, the library came down with a summer virus; stomach sickness swept the eleventh and twelfth floors.

"Index, Harold speaking."

A man who wanted to know what he had on microwave ovens. The political side of it.

"I don't follow. The political side?"

The caller explained that radioactivity coming up through the floor from the microwave in the apartment below was sapping his energy and mental processes. He kept losing his train of thought; he'd think of something he'd been doing and couldn't remember why he'd been doing it, or what made him stop. And it wasn't just him, mental processes were being sapped all over the country, which had to affect democracy and the quality of the schools.

Harold put him on hold and came back with titles on microwaves.

"Here you go. Got a pen? February 20, 1990, Microwave ovens in most households, more and more microwaveable foods are aimed at children — that would address the schools; October 12, 1979, Microwaves discussed in controversy over division of radio spectrum; July 20, 1978, Discussed in report on pollution from electromagnetic radiation. Okay, this is what you want. Feb 29, March 30, July 17, all 1976, we've got Soviets beaming harmful radioactive microwaves at the U.S. embassy in Moscow. By the way, I've heard that aluminum foil blocks radioactivity. Have you tried putting sheets of aluminum foil on your floor?"

He had not.

"There are those jumbo rolls, you could probably cover the whole kitchen with a box of those."

He would definitely try it, he would! The caller thanked Harold profusely, and hung up.

Harold felt sick.

Harold, who never never stayed home, stayed home the next morning. He'd woken up nauseated, dressed, walked to the subway stop, turned and walked home.

He considered his character. He had been loyal, he had worked hard, he had been absolutely reliable and relied on loyalty in return — he'd been a fool.

Reva called and insisted he drink so he didn't dehydrate. He didn't want to drink. Would he like her to come over after work? She could bring him some soup . . . Harold said, then you'll be sick, Reva said she'd already been exposed, but Harold could not be persuaded. This was not the way he wanted Reva to see his home.

Earl called while he was on the toilet, where he'd been spending most of his time. Earl he heard over the answering machine.

"Where are you? Are you sleeping? Lord, this is godawful. Meredith would you believe is insisting that we ran a side view of John Paul I, the one-month Pope. I've looked through all four issues and he's not there. Not from the side."

Harold, with slack bowels, remained on his throne.

Five minutes later, his phone rang again. Rang, not chirped, at home; he owned among the last of the ringing phones.

"Harold. Are you sleeping? Harold. Harold."

Let him squirm. Let him squirm.

Click.

Harold sat in peace.

Third call.

"You have chosen exactly the worst day in creation to be ill. Harold. Harold! This is not do-able by one man alone. They are insisting. They are saying it must be there and it is not, and they are getting on my nerves. I don't want my name associated with this lunacy. I don't want him saying that Earl Darling couldn't do it. This is quite too too much. Harold! Harold, would you please wake up!"

Harold remained Harold, but stopped being poor Harold. He got some luck.

Earl's failure had been brought by Meredith's secretary to Ed's attention. Ed understood that Earl had been asked to do the impossible. Still.

Ed provided a solution. He would promote Earl to assistant editor in Letters, a move that pared the Index to its one essential staffer, Harold. The people in Letters knew Earl; they were the ones who called the Index and hung up when Earl answered. No matter.

Harold as chief indexer came on the masthead on the second tier, senior editorial assistant.

It was November 5, 1994, a cold and crisp morning, when his name appeared on the masthead. Harold Rich, at the end of his line, at the bottom, but on. Right below Reva's.

Reva treated him to a sushi lunch, after which they returned to his now-private office, stomachs warmed by sake, and Harold showed her his favorite covers from the '50s.

In a new silk emerald cocktail dress with sweetheart neckline and shoes dyed to match — she displayed her loot over two lunches — Reva accompanied Steve to a Christmas function. Harold got a call past 11:30.

"What is it? What happened?"

"I got hives. At the party. All over my face, my eyelids blew up I could barely see. He was so mean. He was so mean, he said I was sabotaging him."

"He thinks you got hives on purpose?"

"He said I always do something to ruin his functions, that I don't want him to succeed. He thinks they're psychological."

"He's psychological."

Reva began to choke. Harold heard noises.

"Should I come over? I can be there in an hour."

"No."

"I can't stand you crying on the phone."

"I'm sorry."

"Is he still there?"

"No. He went home."

"Then I'll come."

"You're not coming from Queens at midnight. I'm a grownup. I don't want him anymore, Harold. I don't like him."

There was a pause.

"You sound like you've made up your mind."

"It's just when I think of not having him . . . I feel so stuck. I feel like nothing's happening, nothing will ever ever happen to me, I'll stay where I am, I'll just go round and round and round and deeper into the mud."

What could Harold say? It was life she wasn't liking. He thought. He was stoned but he could think.

"You want to change something? You'll change it."

Reva thought. "You'll help me. You won't let me stay stuck?"

"Sure, I'll help."

"It's easier to let Steven be the go-getter. That's why. It's easier."

"Not really."

"What if I screw up?"

"No way."

"I won't screw up?"

"Nope."

"If I try something and maybe it doesn't work, I won't get hurt?"

"Never."

Reva's laugh! Reva appreciated him. "Never?"

"Never."

"Oh Harold. You *are* the High Lama. Boss of paradise."

Harold up in smoke saw his name on the masthead. At the top.

Tippy top of the Himalayas, where all the people who needed him would have no needs unmet, and the vast world below couldn't reach him. Let them answer themselves. Harold's ear tuned to the chirp of live birds. Harold, Keeper of the Index.

The phone rang.

12:07. A wrong number probably.

BrrrRing!

A wrong number who would make him listen to the number dialed or call back and hang up.

BrrrRing! Reva?

BrrrRing! Reva, Reva, calling again.

"Index, Harold speaking." And her giggle pealed up through the valley to Queens.

Could she come? She'd take a cab. She'd come to him.

STEVE YARBROUGH

ARMS
A Personal Essay

"Son," said my father, "you don't need to worry. Every gun I own except one's locked up."

In the dining room, my wife and both of my daughters — they were four and five at the time — were exchanging hugs with my mother. It was the first trip the girls had ever taken to Mississippi. My Polish wife had been here many times, though some years ago, after spending a summer in Indianola, she had sworn she would never set foot in the state again.

But now here we were, back in Mississippi at the end of the spring semester. We had flown from Fresno, where I teach at the local California State University campus. Eva had only agreed to visit my parents again after imposing certain conditions that were intended to restrict my daughters' access to the small arsenal owned by my father.

When Dad visited us, he came armed. He preferred to drive to California rather than fly, perhaps because he considered airport metal detectors to be in direct violation of the second amendment. He would pull up into our driveway in his big yellow Olds and get out carrying his leather shaving bag. He carried it carefully, one end aimed at the ground; the bag contained his Smith and Wesson 9 mm, his favorite handgun. Jammed into the waistband of his underwear was a small derringer that had no trigger guard and would leave the crook between your thumb and forefinger blue if you were fool enough to fire it; that particular weapon was Dad's Maginot line.

While my mother showed the girls into my old room, where they were going to sleep, Dad asked to have a word with me in private.

He led me into his and Mother's bedroom. He'd nailed a 2×4 across the closet door. He'd driven big spikes into the sheetrock.

"They're all in there," he said.

"All of them?"

"All except the 9 mm"

"Where are your clothes?"

"In the attic," he said. He waved an arm in dismissal, indicating the relative unimportance he attached to things like pants and shirts and dresses and blouses. "Come on," he said.

I followed him into the hallway. I was worried about the other handgun. Eva had insisted that every single weapon be under lock and key, and I knew she meant it.

The year we met, she had refused to move in with me until I got rid of the only gun I still owned at that time, a .22 target pistol. She'd gone with me to the pawnshop, to make sure I really sold it. She might have been from Poland, but she already understood a thing or two about Southerners and their guns. I probably could not have hit anything with the .22, but I had held onto it for years. I had kept it, I can see now, as a piece of evidence. I could not do most of the things Southern men were supposed to be so good at. I couldn't work on a car—I didn't know the difference in a water pump and a camshaft. I could not go fishing because I didn't like to handle bait. Though I am big and had played football in college, I was no good at fighting; my capacity for seeing things from my opponent's point of view was far too great. In short, I was every bit as bad a Southerner as Jimmy Carter had ever been. But I did, by God, own a gun.

Dad and I walked into the den. Directly off the den, there's a laundry room. The laundry room is really just a large walk-in closet, also used for storage. At one time my father had kept most of the guns there.

I'd suffered the worst scare of my life in the laundry room. The previous year I had flown to Mississippi to do a reading and a book signing. Those events were in Jackson, but I had set aside one day to drive up into the Delta and see the folks. While I was here, my father had taken me into the laundry room to show me his latest acquisitions, two M1 carbines that somebody had modified to 30-round capacity. They were resting in a rack he'd mounted on the wall. They'd been used by the Israeli military, he said, caressing the sleek black barrel of one. He'd also been fortunate enough to purchase five thousand rounds of .30 caliber ammo.

"What you reckon this is?" he had said that day last year.

A black rain slicker hung from a wall peg. He pulled the slicker aside to reveal a large cardboard box. As it turned out, the box contained the .30 caliber ammo. But at the time, in an effort to summon sarcasm — since guns and gun control, along with race and welfare, have been hot-button topics between my father and me for most of my adult life — I said, "I guess you've got grenades in there."

Like me, my father is a large man — well above six feet tall, and he weighs close to 250. His gestures, though slow, have a grandness about them. He let the rain slicker fall back over the cardboard box. His right arm began, almost imperceptibly, to rise. His hand stretched out, the index finger pointing at a shelf high up the opposite wall.

"My grenades," he said, "are up yonder."

Four fragmentation grenades were lined up on a shelf no more than six inches wide.

Today, he again raised his arm to point at something. Somehow I mastered the urge to jump backwards, to turn and run into the hallway and collect my wife and girls and fly back to California, where the only weapons that might kill us would be wielded by gang members or madmen on overpasses. At least there we could be slain by strangers.

A large upright freezer stands in the laundry room. What Dad wanted to show me was on top of it. It was the fourteen-shot clip from the 9 mm. He pulled it down and waved it at me.

"It'll be up there," he said. "You might note the freezer's about six feet tall. Tosha and Magda are what, about three feet tall?"

"About."

He replaced the clip, turned and walked into the den. The den is a wood-paneled room with bookcases along one wall and, in a corner, next to a sliding glass door that opens into the driveway, the television set. There's a leather sleeper sofa in front of the television set; most nights my father sits on that sofa until midnight, watching CNN or the Weather Channel, often with the sound turned off. What he's really doing is keeping an eye on things.

He bent over and pulled both cushions off the sofa.

"While y'all are here," he said, "this is where I'll be sleeping."

He grasped the handle on the sleeper and pulled it up. The bed unfolded. He reached down into the gap between the head of the bed and the back of the sofa and lifted out the Smith and Wesson. He stuck the grip in my face, so that I could see it contained no clip.

"Empty," he said. "Satisfied?"

He said it as if my satisfaction would somehow be responsible for the end of us all.

When I was a boy, my father and I went hunting only once, and it nearly ended in tragedy. I must have been about five at the time. He had taken me out into the woods near Indianola to go squirrel hunting. In the pickup truck he'd explained that hickory nuts would be falling from the trees along about now, and so we would slip out into the woods and "still-hunt." What this meant, he said, was that we'd find a good place in a thicket to lie in wait, and when we saw the squirrels, we'd shoot them.

He parked the truck on a turnrow, and we got out and walked across somebody's cotton field, toward some woods. At the edge of the woods, he propped his .22 rifle against a tree and turned his back to piss.

You may recall the TV show *Combat*. You may recall that the sergeant, played by the late Vic Morrow, carried a submachine gun when he was out on patrol, and that when he came across "Krauts," he would hold the gun somewhere near his waist and spray the whole area, from left to right, presumably creating future misery in places like Hamburg and Dortmund.

I knew better than to take up the .22 while Dad's back was turned, yet I did it. I knew better than to swing the gun from left to right, like Vic Morrow did on *Combat*, yet I did that too. I knew better than to pull the trigger. And it's fair, I will always maintain, to say that I did not pull the trigger. It was as if the trigger pulled me. But then triggers have a way of doing that, don't they, especially when you're five years old?

The red stain that spread down the back of my father's leg terrified me. I threw the gun down and began to scream. Dad himself was quiet. He looked over his shoulder — at me, at the .22 lying there among the brown leaves, then at the back of his thigh.

"You shot Daddy," he said.

It was not a bad wound, the bullet had merely grazed his leg. You could argue that if I hadn't shot him, he might have taken me hunting more often, but I don't think so. I don't think he enjoyed hunting that much himself. Because he didn't, I grew up without the experiences that so many boys, particularly in the South, have; I have not tromped through undergrowth on cold mornings with my father, searching for the perfect deer stand, and as a consequence I have always felt a bit disadvantaged, being a Southerner who is also a fiction writer. I can no more write about the hunt than I can a lunar landing; my stories tend to take place indoors, frequently in motel rooms, and the main characters are, as often as not, women.

It's a normal enough thing for a Southern male to love his gun. But my father's attachment to his weaponry was born not of love for guns or hunting. It was born of fear.

Indianola, the town where my father lives, is the seat of Sunflower County, and Sunflower County is in the middle of the Mississippi Delta. Since the annexation of the Southgate subdivision in 1987 — by order of the Federal Courts — the population of Indianola has been roughly 65 percent African American. Sunflower County's population is about 60 percent African American. More than half of the people living in the Delta, a seven thousand square mile area that includes all of ten counties and parts of two others, are black.

All ten Delta counties are among the 100 poorest counties in the United States. Though the housing conditions of Delta blacks are much better than they were when I was growing up in the 60s and early 70s, some of the places they are forced to live can shock an outsider — or an insider who has been away for a while. In the countryside, you will still find shotgun houses with no running water, where as many as ten or twelve people live. The houses have tin roofs that make excellent heat conductors in the stifling Delta summers, and the chinks in the walls allow free passage of icy wind in December and January.

Every white person from the Delta — and I am no exception — goes to sleep at night knowing that at some point in his life he has participated in the humiliation of a black person. In many cases, certainly, the acts of humiliation were committed unwillingly or in ignorance, the simple result of being white and functioning as a thread in the Delta's economic and social fabric. In many more cases they were not.

Whites who live in the Delta are well-aware that they're outnumbered. All the way back to Reconstruction, when Nathan Bedford Forrest, the founder of the Ku Klux Klan, killed a freedman with an ax on one of his Delta Plantations, shortly after the man had threatened an insurrection, whites have feared the day when blacks would arm themselves and — this is generally the way it's said — "take us over." Whites in the Delta, therefore, have always been armed. But they have never felt the need for arms more acutely than they feel it now.

During the past seventy-five years there have been several major waves of black migration from the Delta. When I was growing up, almost all of the black children I knew had a relative or two who had left the Delta for Chicago or Detroit. In many instances, these people found jobs in manufacturing. But in the late seventies and early eighties, as factories cut back or closed down, a lot of people who'd left the Delta when they were young found themselves coming back. Often they brought with them teenage children who'd learned how to survive in urban conditions very different from those in a little town like Indianola.

The kids know what weapons can do. They know which ones are most useful, and they know how to acquire them. They also know the importance of numbers. There are several different gangs in the Southgate subdivision. The gangs are well-armed. The Indianola police department has seized all kinds of semi-automatic handguns from gang members, as well a frighteningly large number of assault rifles.

As a general rule, the gang members shoot one another, for the very same reasons that gang members in L.A. or Fresno shoot one another. They're defending their turf, protecting their exclusive rights to sell drugs in a certain part of town. When gun battles break out in Southgate, local police have said, officers usually just wait until the shooting stops and then go in and see who's dead. "It's actually to our advantage," one officer told me, "to let 'em go ahead and thin one another out."

But as is the case everywhere else, the gangs occasionally kill people who happen to be in the wrong place at the wrong time.

Two years ago, a fourteen-year-old boy who police said had never been involved in gang activity was walking up B. B. King Road to Gentry High School. Directly in front of him was another kid. The second kid had a .22 pistol in his backpack. Police said he later told them he carried it to school every day — he was his gang's enforcer, the man who'd deal with any problems that might arise in the classroom. The contents of his backpack shifted, and somehow the pistol went off. The bullet struck the first boy in the neck, severing his windpipe.

The older brother of the boy who'd been struck by that bullet from the .22 began to carry a handgun of his own. He worked with his father on a small farm right outside the city limits. The father rode to the fields every day with a shotgun lying on his truck seat. A few months after the younger son had been shot by accident and left in critical condition, the father and the older son had an argument in the field. The older son got hot and tired driving his tractor; he parked it and climbed down and walked over to the truck, where his father stood drinking water. Later, the father said his son had told him he didn't feel like working any more that day. He said he'd had enough. The father said the older son reached toward his rear pocket, where he sometimes carried his handgun. It was all an accident, the father said, and the picture of him that was published in the *Enterprise-Tocsin* confirmed that he was grief-stricken, standing there in the hospital waiting room. He'd picked up the shotgun by reflex, he said, he didn't even remember squeezing the trigger. His older son, who as it turned out was not armed that day, took the blast in the chest. He died on a hospital gurney, down the hall from the room where his brother lay doing his best to breathe.

Any number of morals could be drawn from this story, and perhaps my father and some of the men he buys arms with — all of whom, by the way, are basically decent, honest people — could have considered them had it not been for one overwhelming fact. All of the participants in this tragedy were black.

And all of them, except the first victim, had guns.

Our visit to my parents was progressing well enough. By staying out of the den, I managed to avoid discussions of politics with my father — discussions, I might add, that would have been exceedingly unpleasant, what with Bill Clinton, whom my father referred to as Big Foot, in the White House. As far as Eva and I could tell, Dad had not used the *N* word in front of the girls. No explosions had occurred in the closet behind the 2 × 4, and the temperature had not yet risen above ninety. On the whole, it had been a nice trip back. The only real problem was lack of sleep.

The first time I heard the police scanner, I thought I was dreaming. I thought I was having a dream in which, for some reason I could not imagine, I was a deputy sheriff, engaged in high-speed pursuit of a red Ford Taurus on Highway 448. I thought I was dreaming that at some point in the middle of the night, another deputy sheriff was saying to me *Can you read the subject's license plate?* I could not imagine why I'd have such a dream, but I knew that I was not a deputy sheriff and yet someone was addressing me as if I were; and so it must be a dream. Then I realized I was awake.

The police scanner, which I had apparently failed to notice on my few trips through the den, was on a shelf beside my father's desk. The distance between the couch he slept on and the laundry room, where the clip for the 9 mm lay on top of the upright freezer, had simply been too great for Dad to rest easy. And so, shortly after our arrival, he'd gone out and purchased the scanner.

During the time we were there, he kept it off until he went to bed, though now it stays on around the clock. While Eva and I lay rigidly awaiting the next burst of static, my father slept peacefully, secure in the knowledge that his early warning system would afford him ample time to arm himself should he need to.

One night near the end of our visit, I gave up trying to sleep at all. I slipped out of bed, put on my bathrobe and took a book into the bathroom. I sat down with it on the side of the bathtub. It was one of James Lee Burke's Dave Robicheaux novels. So help me God, Dave had just wasted half the French Quarter with his .45 when, from down the hall, I heard the scanner crackle.

"We got a report of a burglary on Gillespie Drive," somebody was saying. "Neighbor says she just saw two black males come out of the house next door, and one of them was toting what looked like a sawed-off shotgun."

A heavy glass object — a lamp, as it turned out — crashed to the floor. I was on my feet already, reaching for the bathroom door. I heard something else — the coffee table — go over, and then the sound of 250 pounds of flesh smacking the wall.

I was in the kitchen when I heard him slide the clip into the Smith and Wesson. I had started my advance through the dining room when it occurred to me that this might be unwise. And so, like General Lee on the bloody fields of Virginia, I staged a flanking movement, circling through the living room. Mother lay asleep there. Passing her, I saw that she'd pulled pillows up on both sides of her head to muffle the nightly noise.

"Dad?" I said.

The den was dark. Cautiously I leaned into the room and groped for the light switch. I flipped it on.

He was crouching in his underwear. He'd hunkered down behind the sleeper sofa as if it were a barricade. He held the 9 mm. in his right hand. He was sighting down the barrel out the sliding glass door at the driveway and, beyond that, the street. He was ready for whatever came at him and the people he loved and feared for. He was ready for everything except the light.

I had never seen my father move so fast. He whirled on me, never leaving his crouch. He whirled. And as he whirled I felt a thousand volt charge hit my heart. While my wife and daughters lay in bed down the hall and my mother slept a few feet away, I stood there frozen, my eyes locked with my father's.

PAUL FRANKS

THE DEMYSTIFICATION OF DEMYSTIFICATION: DERRIDA UPON KANT

Raising the Tone of Philosophy: Late Essays by Immanuel Kant,
Transformative Critique by Jacques Derrida. Edited by Peter
Fenves. Baltimore: Johns Hopkins University Press, 1993. Pp.
208. $28.95 (hb).

It is a significant fact of twentieth-century intellectual life that there are
two distinct ways or cultures of philosophizing—known as analytic and
continental philosophy—and that they view each other, for the most
part, with distrust and incomprehension. To the analytically inclined
philosophers who predominate in English-speaking philosophy departments, contintental idioms such as deconstruction—as exemplified in
the practice of Jacques Derrida—are likely to sound not only obscure
but willfully obscurantist. Indeed, opponents of Derrida have accused
him of cultivating and encouraging a playfully paradoxical and hope-
lessly obscure mode of thought that allows its practitioners to elevate
themselves above the usual risks of rational debate and intellectual
challenge. Although Derrida is an eminent French philosopher, his
influence is far more visible in English-speaking literature departments
than in philosophy departments, and analytic philosophers might find
this appropriate on the grounds that deconstruction sounds to them like
poetic word-play and not like the rigorous philosophical work of clarification that they admire in philosophers of logic and language such as
Frege, Russell, and Quine.

It may therefore be surprising to find Derrida juxtaposed to Kant in
Fenves's fascinating volume. For Kant, the great eighteenth-century

German philosopher, is one of the very few thinkers whose work remains at the center of discussion in both continental and analytic traditions. And Kant is an enthusiastic, if critical, advocate of the *Aufklärung* or Enlightenment, whose values of rationality, clarity, and universal intelligibility Derrida has been accused of undermining. Indeed, in the two 1796 essays translated here — "On a Newly Arisen Superior Tone in Philosophy" and "Announcement of the Near Conclusion of a Treaty for Eternal Peace in Philosophy" — Kant polemicizes against the elitist obscurantism of a certain poetically inclined clique who may remind the unsympathetic of today's deconstructionists. Yet this volume also contains the translation of a 1980 conference address entitled "On a Newly Arisen Apocalyptic Tone in Philosophy" in which Derrida declares, in the course of a rich and insightful commentary on Kant's essays, "We cannot and we must not — this is a law and a destiny — forgo the *Aufklärung*, in other words, what imposes itself as the enigmatic desire for vigilance, for the lucid vigil, for elucidation, for critique and truth. . . ."[1] Derrida's profession of allegiance is enabled in part by the fact that Kant does not simply reject the obscurantism of his contemporary opponents, but also insists that a certain *necessary obscurity* or — to invoke, along with Kant, a cluster of themes and traditions that can be traced back to ancient philosophical responses to the Greek mystery religions — a certain *mystery* or *esotericism* remains essential to philosophy even after the Kantian revolution. Analytic philosophy cannot fail to be suspicious of the idea that necessary obscurity infects a discipline so centrally concerned with demystification and the attainment of clarity. But the aspect of Kant's thought manifest in this volume illuminates some features of his philosophy to which analytic philosophers already ascribe significance, such as his strategy for the justification of freedom of the will and morality. And we are also helped to see how Derrida can understand his work, in its exploration of the limits of intelligibility, as one way of inheriting Kant's version of the Enlightenment.

Kant wrote these two essays in response to an attack by Johann Georg Schlosser, administrator, poet, and brother-in-law of Goethe. Schlosser had attacked Kant in the introduction and notes to the first German translation of Plato's correspondence, a translation undertaken by Schlosser for more than scholarly reasons. He was one of the many Germans who supported the French revolution in its early stages but quickly grew disillusioned and finally turned bitterly against the revolution when the King was executed. By translating Plato's letters, Schlosser sought to justify his withdrawal from politics by recalling the disastrous involvement in the Syracusan revolution that led Plato to abandon the dream of establishing an ideal state ruled by a philosopher-king. This volume is constructed, then, upon a double claim of historical relevance: as the Syracusan revolution was of relevance to the French revolution, so the cultural wars surrounding the revolution in Germany in the 1790s are of relevance to the cultural wars of today. In both cases the relevance is, of course, oblique, but suggestive nonetheless.

Schlosser's attack on Kant did not occur, then, in the usual philosophical article or treatise. His criticisms — or, to be more accurate, his insults — occurred mainly in his annotations to Plato's *Seventh Letter*, which famously digresses from Syracusan politics in order to give an account of the *esoteric* nature of Plato's theory of ideas. According to that account, only an elite, "divinely gifted"[2] with a special faculty of vision or intuition, are capable of philosophical knowledge. Such knowledge — of the divine ideas that are ontologically prior to the derivative and inadequate imitations that we ordinarily call *real* objects — can be acquired only through a prolonged and collective investigation of the limits and inadequacies of all the ordinary instruments of knowledge. Only after the experience of a thoroughgoing skepticism about ordinary knowledge, and in a moment of "conversion", can philosophy be "brought to birth in the soul on a sudden, as light that is kindled by a leaping spark."[3] The *Letter* considers it not only pointless but also dangerous to speak publicly about philosophy — for example, by composing a philosophical treatise — because the masses were likely to ridicule what they cannot understand or, still worse, to imitate the obscure idiom of the philosophical elite, "as though they had learnt some sublime mysteries."[4] In Schlosser's view, true philosophical wisdom was to be found in the sublime poetic images of this elitist esotericism. Indeed, Schlosser declares that if Plato were alive in the 1790s he would have directed his reproach toward the new Kantian philosophy, which, by emphasizing discursive clarity and cognitive certainty over poetic image and felt conviction, had "emasculated" reason, leaving it aesthetically and morally impotent. Instead of wasting their time on Kant's three *Critiques*, Schlosser thought the young should read classical literature, cultivate their aesthetic sensibilities and hope for a "presentiment" of the veiled goddess Isis. Kant's determination to clip the wings of philosophical speculation could be easily explained: evidently the sage of Königsberg lacked the requisite divinity of soul and was incurably blind to the truth and beauty of metaphysics.

It is surprising that Kant bothered to respond to these remarks. In 1796 Kant was at the peak of his fame and hundreds of articles and books were being written about his philosophy throughout Germany. He was already growing old and, in his efforts to complete his philosophical labors, he mostly avoided controversy. Why, then, did he respond to these barbs, written in footnotes and without argument by a man of only moderate importance? Significantly, Schlosser's attack was not considered worthy of translation either by the first translator of Kant's response (John Richardson in his 1799 *Essays and Treatises by Emmanuel Kant*, recently reprinted) or by Fenves.

One subterranean reason for Kant's response is his unwavering enthusiasm for the French revolution (which coexisted uneasily with his philosophical refusal to grant legitimacy to revolutions in general). Although Kant makes no explicit reference to politics, he criticizes Schlosser for his "superior tone" and argues that his elitist obscurantism is motivated by "vanity" and a disdain for philosophical labor, criticisms that have obvious political and social undertones. As Derrida remarks, "The hierarchized opposition of gift to work, of intuition to concept, of genius' mode to scholar's mode (*geniemässig/schulmässig*) . . . is homologous to the opposition between aristocracy and democracy, eventually between demagogic oligarchy and authentic rational democracy."[5] (A second reason for Kant's response is that he found Schlosser's criticism of his literary style significantly irrelevant, the symptom of a serious misunderstanding of the very nature of philosophy:

> At bottom, all philosophy is indeed prosaic; and the suggestion that we should now start to philosophize poetically would be just as welcome as the suggestion that a businessman should in the future no longer write his account books in prose but rather in verse.[6]

Kant is already responding to one aspect of what would come to be called Romanticism: an aestheticism often accompanied by a conservative reaction to the French revolution. In Derrida's words, "This cryptopolitics is also a cryptopoetics, a poetic perversion of philosophy."[7] And what concerns Kant most of all is that Schlosserian poetry dares to conceal itself behind the banner of philosophy. The victory of Schlosser's party would in fact constitute what Kant twice calls "the death of all philosophy," because the appeal to a mystical "presentiment" or to "secrets that can be felt" amounts to a self-exemption from rational discourse, an effortless establishment of uncontestable authority:

> The principle of wanting to philosophize under the influence of a higher *feeling* is, among all principles, the one best suited to produce a superior tone. For who will contest my own feelings? If I can make it credible that this feeling is not merely subjective *in me* but can be demanded of everyone and is therefore held to be objectively valid and rationalized as a piece of knowledge, therefore not as a mere concept but as an intuition (apprehension of the object itself) — if I can make this credible, I have a great advantage over those who must first justify themselves before they are allowed to celebrate the truth of their assertions. I can henceforth speak in the tone of a lord who is so lofty as to be exempted from the burden of proving the title of his property *(beati possidentes)*.[8]

If one is unsympathetic to deconstruction, it can seem irresistible to think of its practitioners as merely the latest embodiment of this perennial tendency to irrational mystagoguery. And there can be no doubt that Derrida was counting on just this association in choosing Kant's essay as his text.

There is a third reason for Kant's response to Schlosser, and here matters begin to become more complicated. Kant is clearly disturbed by the suggestion that Schlosser is the true heir of Plato, whose term "idea" Kant had invoked in the *Critique of Pure Reason*, along with the famous remark "that it is by no means unusual, upon comparing the thoughts which an author has expressed in regard to his subject, whether in ordinary conversation or in writing, to find that we understand him better than he has understood himself."[9] Kant is so disturbed by this suggestion that he denies the authenticity of the *Seventh Letter* on the grounds that Plato simply could not have been an elitist obscurantist, thus opening a bitter and still continuing debate about the *Letter*'s authenticity. But, although Kant attributes the *Letter* to a "pseudo-Plato," he does not reject its esotericism as a straightforward fraud: "Plato the *academic* was, therefore, although it was not his fault . . . the father of all exaltation in *philosophy*."[10] What Kant means is that Plato fathered philosophical exaltation (*Schwärmerei* — usually translated "fanaticism") — including the elitist esotericism of the pseudo-Platonic *Seventh Letter* — because Plato gave philosophical centrality to the immediate self-presence of the divine mind, which could not be discursively described and therefore could only be poetically evoked. However, the birth of philosophical exaltation was not Plato's fault, because he invoked the divine mind only *retrospectively*, in order to account for the *a priori* yet synthetic character of mathematical truth. In Plato's view, our ability to arrive at mathematical truths that are both *a priori* (true *independently* of the world) and *synthetic* (true *of* the world) could best be explained mythically: divine souls, originating in the divine mind, have been trapped in these earthly bodies and we can only attain an obscure recollection of the divine ideas which our souls intuited before their earthly imprisonment began. But although Plato appealed to these intuitions retrospectively to explain the mathematical knowledge we all already possess, he did not — like the pseudo-Plato admired by Schlosser — make *prospective* use of these intuitions in order to acquire metaphysical knowledge accessible only to souls blessed with a special degree of divinity.

So Kant does not simply reject the pseudo-philosophy of *Seventh Letter* esotericism as wholly alien to philosophy. For Plato made that pseudo-philosophy possible in the course of his founding (if ultimately unsuccessful) attempt to answer what Kant himself considers the central philosophical question: "How are synthetic *a priori* judgments possible?" But Kant's relationship to *Seventh Letter* esotericism is still more complex than this. For in his view what elitist obscurantists like Schlosser *say* is, in a way, philosophically justified and perhaps even necessary. What is problematic is *only* — a qualification whose weight is difficult to assess — the *tone* in which they say it. For it emerges that Kant thinks philosophy — even the transcendental idealism he advocates — is indeed esoteric: at its heart lies a "secret that *can be felt*", a secret that is constituted by "reason's inner Idea of freedom" and that is given *a priori* as the basis for metaphysical knowledge ("but only from a practical point of view").[11] And those who merit initiation into this secret have a use — and perhaps even a need — for the sublimely obscure, esotericist language of mystery and initiation advocated by Schlosser. Kant goes so far as to declare himself prepared to bend his knee and to join Schlosser in worship before the veiled Isis, goddess of the ancient mysteries.[12]

It should be shocking — particularly, but not exclusively, to analytically inclined readers of Kant — to hear Kant speaking this esotericist idiom along with the obscurantists. Although some may dismiss Kant's reintonation of esotericism as a merely rhetorical move, there is reason to think that it sheds great light on central aspects of Kant's thought, especially his views about freedom and morality, while illuminating his aspirations for philosophy in general. Kant is generally portrayed, with considerable justice, as the destroyer of traditional metaphysics — that is, of theology, cosmology, and psychology as *a priori* theories of God, the world, and the soul. What is less generally appreciated is the extent to which Kant, while destroying metaphysics within the domain of *theoretical* philosophy, reconstitutes metaphysics within the realm of *practical* philosophy. In his revolutionary work, the *Critique of Pure Reason*, written some fifteen years before his exchange with Schlosser, Kant already refers to this practical reconstitution of metaphysics as a change in the *tone* in which traditional metaphysical claims are made. Kant argues that our theoretical knowledge is limited to objects of possible experience and that we therefore cannot have theoretical knowledge that God exists, that we are free and not causally determined in our action and that we have immortal souls, for these metaphysical claims concern objects which we could never encounter in experience. But Kant insists that these claims are essential to morality, and that morality is in turn essential to the coherence of the practical point of view — the point of view we take with respect to ourselves insofar as we act and engage in practical deliberation in our everyday lives. So we must continue to make these metaphysical claims, but change our *tone*, from the tone appropriate to the theoretical point of view to the tone appropriate to the practical point of view.[13]

It is not exactly clear what this change of tone entails. The *Critique of Pure Reason* can leave the impression that the practical reintonation of metaphysical claims is tantamount to a diminution of their epistemic status from objective *knowledge* to subjective *belief* or *faith*. But there are reasons to doubt this view, and Kant's *Critique of Practical Reason* (1788) provides conclusive evidence against it. After more than a decade of failed attempts, Kant arrives in his second *Critique* at a deduction or justification of the objective reality of freedom that is to ground the new, practically reintoned metaphysics.[14] The details of this deduction have mainly eluded commentators. In fact some have chosen to declare that Kant does not intend to deduce freedom in this work, despite his explicit statement that that is exactly what he means to do, and despite his later insistence, in the 1790 *Critique of Judgment*, that freedom is the only metaphysical idea that can be called an objectively real idea of a "matter of fact" (*res facti*) because it is the only such idea whose reality can be deduced.[15] But although Kant insists that he has deduced the *objectivity* of freedom, it is important to note that Kant's deduction of freedom is nevertheless peculiarly *first-personal*: it requires me to imagine myself in situations where morality demands that I sacrifice life itself, to reflect on the way morality outweighs all of my sensuous desires and to thereby commit myself to lead a moral life. Now the moral law is, as Kant famously argues, a law that I could only legislate *autonomously* for myself. And the freedom of my will should not be identified with autonomy, or else human beings will be considered unfree and therefore incapable of responsibility when they act heteronomously or out of some immoral motive. Rather, the freedom of the will should be identified with the capacity for choosing to act *either* autonomously *or* heteronomously. So if I succeed in the exercise Kant demands of me, I will *actualize* my capacity to choose autonomy — that is to say, the freedom of my will — and I will thereby convince myself that I am actually free, or that freedom is real. If, however, I fail to take up the required point of view by failing to engage imaginatively with the moral dilemma, or if I refuse to recognize the normative superiority of the moral law and instead adopt some other *heteronomous* way of life — as Kant agrees human beings are free to do — then Kant's deduction will leave me unmoved and unconvinced. So the deduction of freedom depends on the exercise of my imagination and freedom in a way that distinguishes it from, say, deductions in geometry or, for that matter, in theoretical philosophy. The deduction of freedom is, we might say, a *practical* deduction that each of us is free to perform or not to perform and therefore, in a quite specific sense, free to find convincing or unconvincing.

The deduction of freedom therefore has the peculiar character of being an essentially first-personal route to a conviction that is nevertheless objective and not, as one might have expected, subjective. And it is just this peculiar character that underlies Kant's reintonation of esotericism in "On a Superior Tone." In his 1793 *Religion within the Limits of Reason Alone* Kant had defined a secret or mystery (*Geheimnis*) as something *holy* (therefore, he says, in Enlightenment fashion, something moral and rational) "which may indeed be *known* by each single individual but cannot be *made known* publicly, that is, shared universally."[16] Given this characterization of mystery or secrecy and the peculiar character of the practical deduction of freedom, Kant can speak the esotericist idiom in the tone appropriate to the practical point of view. He can say, in his response to Schlosser, that he has uncovered philosophy's "true secret," that "freedom constitutes the secret" and that one encounters this secret in astonishment when one performs the deduction of freedom or when one asks oneself:

> What is in me that makes it so that I can sacrifice the most inner allurements of my drives and all the desires that proceed from my nature to a law that promises me no advantage as a replacement and threatens no loss if it is transgressed; indeed a law that I honor all the more inwardly the more strictly it bids and the less it offers in return?[17]

And once Kant has reintoned the concept of the secret into which one must be initiated, the central concept of esotericism from the time of the ancient mysteries to the time of Schlosser, he can easily reintone Schlosser's other esotericist terms. Thus when Schlosser proclaims himself privy to a "presentiment of the veiled goddess Isis," Kant does not reject his claim, but reinterprets it. He identifies the goddess with the sublime moral law — veiled forever from our theoretical knowledge — and ascribes to Schlosser a feeling of respect for the law which is genuine, yet inadequately conceptualized, and is therefore an obscure *pre*sentiment.

Kant's reworked esotericism is decisively different from the *Seventh Letter* esotericism championed by Schlosser. First, the secret of *Seventh Letter* esotericism is primarily *theological*: it is constituted by the ideas in the divine mind; to know the secret is therefore to know the perfect self-presence of God. In contrast, the secret of Kantian esotericism is primarily *cosmological*: it is constituted by the idea of a free agent who occupies not only the natural world of science and desire but also the moral world of reason; to know the secret is therefore to know the divided condition of the human. Second, and consequently, *Seventh Letter* esotericism is elitist whereas Kantian esotericism is egalitarian. While the former is concerned with a divine secret that demands superhuman gifts, the latter is concerned with an essentially human secret that demands nothing more than humanity — and the hard work of conceptualization shirked by obscurantists like Schlosser. In principle, the secret of Kant's metaphysics is accessible to all.

But, despite this decisive difference, Kant retains the language of Schlosser's esotericism, offering him carefully reintoned versions of his cherished poetic expressions. In this way Kant redeems even the obscurantism of a pseudo-Plato as a moment in humanity's development toward a true understanding of freedom. In a parenthesis that one might easily miss, Kant explains the urge to speak in a superior tone in terms of "the vanity of human beings (a misunderstood freedom)".[18] If the vanity of obscurantists is a *mis*understood freedom then it must be an expression — albeit a distorted expression — of the freedom essential to human beings that the Kantian philosophy takes itself to express adequately for the first time. And so one may hope that these obscurantists will recognize the true expression of the freedom they have been groping obscurely to express. Kant's practical reintonation of esotericist terms — like his practical reintonation of the ideas of traditional metaphysics — is therefore intended to provide those terms with their proper use, with the use that will clear away the metaphysical confusions that have beset philosophy since its inception in ancient Greece. It is not that Kant clears up confusion by *answering* age-old questions like the question of the freedom of the will. Rather, he suggests that we stop asking such questions in the tone appropriate to theoretical knowledge, for we will never find theoretically satisfying answers. Instead he recommends that we ask the same questions in the tone appropriate to our practical conviction in our own individual freedom as agents, in which case our questions will meet with satisfying practical responses. From the practical point of view we can attain conviction that we are free and we can convert theoretical doubt about our freedom into a sublime wonder that moves us to redouble our commitment to the moral life. To generations of philosophers it seemed that there was an intractable theoretical puzzle about freedom and determinism, a puzzle whose resolution seemed to some to require a divine insight granted only to a few. Now freedom turns out to be a sacred mystery that plays a crucial role in everyday moral practice, a mystery which nobody can solve theoretically but of which every one of us can claim intimate knowledge, a knowledge we possess merely in virtue of our shared humanity.

Kant's reintonation of traditional metaphysics and of esotericism plays a crucial role in the proposal for a permanent peace in philosophy that he makes in his second response to Schlosser. On the one hand, philosophers are to recognize the impossibility of ever resolving their metaphysical disputes theoretically. On the other, they are to find that they can now make their metaphysical claims with full conviction as long as they adopt an appropriately practical tone.

Nobody needs to be excluded from the settlement because every claim can be accommodated: the skeptics are right to challenge philosophy's claim to theoretical certainty; the metaphysicians are right to affirm the actuality of freedom, God, and the soul; and the esotericists are right to celebrate the mystery of metaphysical conviction in their poetic language. Every party can take credit for its distinctive insight, because Kant's change in tone removes the appearance that the insights conflict.

But what is tone? And if the tone of obscurantist esotericism is superior, how should we characterize the new tone of Kant's esotericism? As Derrida notes, Kant does not directly address the first question since he does not analyze "the pure phenomenon of a tonality"[19] but only denounces a particular, inappropriate tone. Fenves investigates the treatment of tone throughout the Kantian corpus, demonstrating the extreme difficulties Kant encountered whenever he dealt with the notion. Without attempting to engage all those texts here, it seems clear that tone in this context is connected to the matter of how — on what basis or with what right — one takes oneself to be entitled to speak to and for others. Those who speak, like Schlosser, in a superior tone claim the right to speak on the basis of an extraordinary gift that makes them privy to mysterious feelings which, as private, can be interpreted arbitrarily and cannot be subjected to intellectual challenge. Kant, however, claims the right to speak on the basis of no more than common humanity plus the labor of conceptualization, and therefore exposes himself to the challenges of other fellow humans, who have no lesser basis.

But this distinction must be less clear than Kant suggests, for he wants to contrast the arbitrariness of the obscurantists' oracular voice with the *unequivocal clarity* of the voice of reason. And there must surely be room for questions of interpretation even here, for there is no prospect of our ever exhausting the interpretative possibilities of Kant's or any other major philosopher's understanding of reason. That Kant is underestimating the obscurities into which he has plunged is also clear from the inadequacy of his characterization of his own tone as "veridical."[20] Even if one thinks Kant is just telling the truth about human freedom, one should still be unsatisfied by the mere suggestion that those who, like Schlosser, fail to recognize that truth are *lying* either to themselves or to others. For we need an account of what attracts Schlosser to his misunderstood freedom even in the face of an adequately conceptualized freedom. We need to explain what resists the truth and makes it hard to accept.

The underlying theme of Derrida's contribution to this volume is the idea that Kant may be heard to speak in an *apocalyptic* tone, a tone signifying that one claims the right to speak on the basis of one's knowledge of an imminent and final disclosure that will — at last — end all disagreements and clarify all confusions. But this provocative suggestion — developed by means of a rich web of allusions to ancient apocalyptic literature as well as to Derrida's other works — is not meant to capture Kant's difference, because it is meant to apply to Schlosser as well. Schlosser writes on the presumption that the end of philosophy has already occurred in the works of Plato, while Kant writes on the presumption that the end of philosophy is about to occur, thanks to his own philosophical revolution. But we of the late twentieth century — "we *Aufklärer* of modern times"[21] — know by now not only that such apocalyptic disclosures have not arrived but also that they never arrive. And so Kant turns out not only to consciously appropriate Schlosser's esotericism but also to unwittingly appropriate Schlosser's apocalyptic tone as well. Kant's promise of philosophical peace stands in need of Derrida's demystification, just as Kant found it necessary to demystify Schlosser's assurance that the end of philosophy occurred long ago and was noticed only by a lucky few.

As demystification, as a critique of the spurious clarities we have been falsely promised, Derrida's deconstruction inherits the Enlightenment project. But, as Derrida points out, his demystificational intent implies that he too cannot help but speak in an apocalyptic tone, promising an ultimate clarity that will never arrive. There is, he thinks, no way out, and his attempts at self-consciousness and irony have, he notes, been ineffective, especially in the United States.[22] But we must not abandon the apocalyptic tone of the Enlightenment because of this apparent impasse. Rather, we must be scrupulous in undertaking the demystification of demystification, the deconstruction of ourselves as *Aufklärer*. We must be vigilant in asking "where they want to come to, and to what ends, those who declare the end of this or that, of man or the subject, of consciousness, of history, of the West or of literature, and according to the latest news, of progress itself, the idea of which has never been in such bad health to the right and the left?"[23] And this must surely mean — Derrida must surely intend to mean — that we are not only entitled but obliged to ask after the end of deconstruction itself.

Deconstruction is intended, then, to demystify demystification or to enlighten the Enlightenment about its own unavoidable obscurities. It is a self-critique of the Enlightenment's promise of final clarity, for which Kant prepared the way by acknowledging the unavoidable mystery and obscurity of his own Enlightenment philosophy of freedom. To oppose obscurantism to Enlightenment would, then, be simplistic indeed. As Derrida puts it, "Each of us is the mystagogue *and* the *Aufklärer* of another."[24] Of course, this is hardly likely to placate Derrida's implacable foes, who will see his attempt to complicate the issue merely as another piece of mystification, an attempt to reduce rational discourse to skeptical puzzlement and paradox. But Derrida's inheritance of Kant's tone can be seen as a welcome call for self-criticism and as a genuine attempt to raise a question about the philosophical value of clarity, a question that the analytic tradition — with a number of notable exceptions — almost invariably ignores.

One of the pitfalls of Enlightenment projects of demystification is that demystifiers can easily come to think they know the end of the story before they have heard the details of the plot — that a single demystificational diagnosis, or a finite set of diagnoses, is enough to demystify any philosophy one might conceivably encounter. To think this is, however, to place oneself securely at the end of philosophy, to claim advance knowledge of the intended end of any philosophy whatsoever, thus to claim an apocalyptic and final clarity for one's own enterprise. Deconstruction — like analytic philosophy itself as an Enlightenment project of demystification — cannot help but run this risk. Fenves seems to fall into the trap when he interprets Kant not only as a significant precursor of Derrida but as a deconstructionist *avant la lettre*. According to Fenves, Kant's announcement of an imminent treaty for eternal peace in philosophy is necessarily self-defeating, and Kant knows it:

> Far from lamenting this situation, Kant welcomes it: the treaty for eternal peace is always only nearing; it is always only coming, it never arrives.[25]

Peace — the end of philosophy Kant announces as imminent — never arrives because no announcement can be atonal, every announcement must have some tone. But tone essentially involves the possibility of *modulation* or *alteration* so tone "is never simply itself; it is, in short, never simple and pure. Even if every modulation is only implicit, even if it is a mere possibility inherent in its uniformity, modulation underlies the ability of tone to be 'itself' . . . ."[26] And the unavoidable tonality of any philosophical peace treaty announcement means that such announcements cannot help but provoke disputes not only about which tone has been raised but also about the very meaning of "tone" — an essentially unstable and therefore perpetually disputable meaning.

This is apt to strike analytic philosophers as a rather poor argument: it is necessarily possible that any tone be modulated or altered; therefore any tone is the tone that it is in virtue of its possible alteration; therefore any tone is itself in virtue of its possibly being other than itself; therefore no tone is ever "simply itself." Why should we draw this paradoxical conclusion? Analytic philosophers have long recognized that color concepts exhibit a similar logic: each color is the color it is only in virtue of its discrimination from and possibility of being shaded into every other. One might choose to express this by saying that color is "never simply itself" — but what profit would be gained by this cultivation of the sound of paradox?

In fact I do not think that Fenves is simply giving a bad argument. Instead, he is presupposing an unstated view about the goal or end of philosophizing: the view that philosophizing aims at an *absolute* determination of the *substance* or wholly *self-dependent* identity of each of its objects. If this view is correct then it follows inexorably that there can be no philosophical account of tone and that no tonal announcement of the completion of philosophy can possibly succeed. But is the view correct? Analytic philosophers will insist on being convinced, thinking the view unnecessarily demanding in its restrictions on what counts as philosophical satisfaction. Deconstructionists will think that Heidegger's and Derrida's readings of the history of philosophy have already shown that philosophy could be satisfied by nothing less than an absolute determination of being as pure self-identity or presence, just the sort of determination that tone — along with other deconstructive concepts like "*timbre (tympanum)*, *style*, and *signature*"[27] — resists. But even if Heidegger and Derrida had shown this through compelling readings of major texts, they could not have revealed in advance the nature of any possible philosophy, unless they could claim to have disclosed — finally and apocalyptically — the end of philosophy as such.

So Fenves hears Kant's tone from the apocalyptic perspective of one who knows the end of philosophy in advance. And he thereby misses Kant's genuine difference from deconstruction. It is true that Kant's peace proposal does not propose the cessation of philosophical dispute, which would in Kant's view be tantamount to "the sleep of death."[28] But this does not mean that Kant's proposal is, as Fenves suggests, a piece of self-consciously ironic rhetoric. Kant's idea is rather that philosophical confusion and dispute is an essential aspect of humanity—as essential as the divided state of the human self—and is therefore as ineliminable as humanity itself; but the Kantian philosophical revolution enables us, he thinks, to institute a critique that can pacify such disputes when they arise, as they inevitably will, although we can never remove the source of their possibility. Kant promises no absolute end of philosophical dispute, but rather proposes the endless task of ending—by means of a practical reintonation—the confusions that generate those disputes.

Yet, as Derrida or Fenves might rightly insist, Kant thinks that he has reached a terminus from which he can take a finite inventory of possible philosophical confusions and that he can institute a correspondingly finite set of clarificatory responses. So Kant does indeed speak in an apocalyptic tone. At this juncture one might invoke Wittgenstein as a philosopher who inherits Kant's critical legacy while abandoning this last vestige of apocalypse:

> The real discovery is the one that makes me capable of breaking off [*abzubrechen*] in philosophy when I want to. — The one that gives philosophy peace, so that it is no longer tormented by questions which bring *itself* in question . . . Problems are solved (difficulties eliminated), not a *single* problem.[29]

Here Wittgenstein, like Kant, seeks a momentary yet genuine philosophical satisfaction, not an absolute end of philosophizing, which is broken off now only to be resumed later, whenever philosophical questions torment him again. But unlike Kant, Wittgenstein does not (in his later work) claim to have disclosed the nature of philosophical confusion as such and therefore does not claim to know in advance what form philosophical confusion and its clarification might take in the future.[30] Like Derrida, Wittgenstein is suspicious of the apocalyptic tone in which such claims are made, taking confusion and obscurity to be necessary possibilities of the human. But, unlike Derrida, Wittgenstein nevertheless continues to seek genuine, if transient, moments of philosophical satisfaction, clarity, and peace.

Must philosophy's apocalyptic drive to the absolute—which deconstruction thinks both essential and essentially self-defeating—reappear somewhere in Wittgenstein's thinking? Must philosophy seek a final moment of absolute clarity? One might hope for a conversation between analytic and continental philosophy about the nature and value of clarity, about the peculiar economies of demystification and esotericism in their various inheritances of the Enlightenment. But to hope for such a conversation would be to hope for a final, lucid moment of mutual intelligibility—to speak once again in an apocalyptic tone. Perhaps, though, one might hope instead for a multiplicity of such conversations, both analytic and continental, conversations that might fuse in unexpected ways at unpredictable, transient moments. Indeed, one might hope that such conversations will be provoked by this volume and by the shocking idea that Kant acknowledges a necessary obscurity at the very heart of his philosophy. *Raising the Tone of Philosophy* is not only an indispensable text for readers of Kant and Derrida; it also encourages our hopes for that degree of clarity and light which we mere mortals may fleetingly enjoy.

NOTES

[1]Fenves, 148.

[2]"Seventh Letter" in *Plato* (New York: Loeb Classical Library, Heinemann, 1924–7), 340c.

[3]"Seventh Letter," 333e.

[4]"Seventh Letter," 341d-e.

[5]Fenves, 128.

[6]Fenves, 72.

[7]Fenves, 136.

[8]Fenves, 58.

[9]*Critique of Pure Reason*, trans. Norman Kemp Smith (St. Martin's Press: New York, 1965), A313/B370.

[10]Fenves, 62.

[11]Fenves, 68–9.

[12]Fenves, 71.

[13]*Critique of Pure Reason*, A745/B773.

[14]See *Critique of Practical Reason*, trans. Lewis White Beck (Macmillan: New York, 1993), Ak.47–8.

[15]See *Critique of Judgment*, trans. Werner Pluhar (Indianapolis: Hackett, 1987), Ak.468.

[16]*Religion within the Limits of Reason Alone*, trans. T. H. Greene and H. H. Hudson (Harper: New York, 1960), 129.

[17]Fenves, 68.

[18]Fenves, 52.

[19]Fenves, 123.

[20]Fenves, 93.

[21]Fenves, 158.

[22]Fenves, 160.

[23]Fenves, 149.

[24]Fenves, 142.

[25]Fenves, 27.

[26]Fenves, 21-2.

[27]Fenves, 36.

[28]Fenves, 87.

[29]*Philosophical Investigations*, trans. G. E. M. Anscombe (Blackwell: Oxford, 1953), section 133 (translation altered).

[30]See for example, *Zettel*, trans. G. E. M. Anscombe (Blackwell: Oxford, 1967), section 447. This aspect of Wittgenstein's thought is widely neglected but has been emphasized recently by Stanley Cavell, Hilary Putnam, and James Conant. See Conant's interview with Cavell in *Senses of Stanley Cavell*, ed. Richard Fleming and Michael Payne (Lewisburg: Bucknell University Press, 1989), 47-8, and Conant's introduction to Putnam, *Realism with a Human Face* (Cambridge Mass: Harvard University Press, 1990), xli.

F. D. REEVE

MAKING IT NEWER

M-80. By Jim Daniels. Pittsburgh: University of Pittsburgh Press, 1993. Pp. 86. $19.95 (hb), $10.95 (pb).

Incontinence. By Susan Hahn. Chicago: University of Chicago Press, 1993. Pp. 83. $8.95 (pb).

Bright Existence. By Brenda Hillman. Hanover and London: Wesleyan University Press / University Press of New England, 1993. Pp. 99. $22.50 (hb), $10.95 (pb).

Windows. By Jay Meek. Pittsburgh: Carnegie-Mellon University Press, 1994. Pp. 63. $10.95 (pb).

Collected Poems, 1953–1993. By John Updike. New York: Alfred A. Knopf, 1993. Pp. 387. $27.50 (hb).

If we break down the spectrum of styles these books present, we run the risk of altering each distinctive color. Another way of putting it: to each poet-passenger, an omnibus review must seem unfair, for poets, more intensely than others, are like the vetch and lupine of Brenda Hillman's "Small Spaces," which

> combine to think it through, too many
> get ready and a few die daily to fill the spaces —
> stem after short stem —
>
> though the earth tried to hold each one of them upright,
> saying don't imagine don't imagine
> there has been another like you —

And of course there has not been. Even if John Updike's book has 17% more pages than the other four books combined, is divided into "light verse" and "poems" according to a poem's derivation "from the real (the given, the substantial) world" and offers what he calls his "oeuvre's beloved waifs," it is in no way more idiosyncratic. In a sense, all his poems are light, and the dark-suited, white-haired gentleman sipping tea on the dust jacket, who might well have translated oeuvre as "work" or "works" the way the dictionaries do, is an establishment figure from whom other poets take their literary departure. Arranged chronologically, his poems come to the personal but scarcely credible skepticism in "Academy," a sonnet composed several years ago when he was 60. It contrasts the early life of literary ambition and public effort to the comfort of membership in the American Academy of Arts and Letters:

> A struggle it was, and a dream; we wake
> to bright, bald honors. Tell us our mistake.

Indirectly, Jim Daniels does. But the mistakes he enumerates and the consequences he points to win no honors. The great hope for creating the democratic, American working-class culture that Whitman called for, raised in the early 1930s by the exceptional talents of the miner-carman-worker-novelist-intellectual Jack Conroy and the radical young writers grouped around him such as Meridel Le Sueur, Joseph Kalar and H. H. Lewis dissipated after the American Writers' Congress of 1935 when the Party re-oriented itself on Moscow, East Coast intellectuals turned to the work of Europeans, and "new critical" standards of autonomy and unity rejected ideological specificity. Conroy viewed "literature as a transforming praxis," Douglas Wixson writes in *Worker-Writer In America*, "a new production aesthetic of critical consciousness aimed at working people, writers and artists, and a decentered system of literary production," but, alas, subsequent literary protests were either too weak to be effective or, like the Beats', too superficial not to be readily absorbed by the prevailing commercialism. Drugs and violence completed the isolation of the unemployed, the unskilled, and the rest of the urban working class.

Daniels's diction is as self-conscious as Updike's but naturalistic, and his line is loose, unmetered, mostly unmusical, as conversational as he can make it. He's kicking and pushing an intractable past into life. In his working-class world, the past has meaning only in the present. Because the working class has no culture of its own and lacks poets whose expressive language could document its difference from the hegemonic culture, it cannot remember who it was or believe what it has achieved. Although its habits, its dress, its speech and its attitudes divorce it from other classes, its religion, its schooling, its aspirations and values continue to melt it into the middle class, who exploit its labor and sell it their goods, services and entertainment. Ironically, ex-working-class Daniels expresses a mostly middle-class view.

"Wild Country," the first part of *M-80*, is no remote section of Alaska but a dozen poems dramatizing the lonely self of an urban Catholic boy who, from the vantage of middle age, well perceives the pointlessness of Crazy Eddie's life:

> We didn't know then
> he picked up trash for a living
> and drank twelve beers a night.
> Maybe all he wanted was a green lawn
> and a peaceful drunk.

That is a long way down the ladder of class consciousness from Jack Conroy's virile unionist and loyal extended-family father who takes responsibility for the future into his own hands. In his poems, Daniels retains his delicate, romantic illusions and his pleasure in perception:

> Those summer days moved slow and thick
> as hot tar. We wanted anything
> that'd speed them up. But even then
> the underground streams were flowing,
> gurgling to the surface
> in remote spots. Universal City
> seemed light years away then,
> and a man with a gun crying over a woman
> was a man from another planet,
> a faint speck in the distant sky.

But crucial experiences fall into stereotype — we get male bonding, the masculine assertiveness of the intellectually modest —

> Ah, heart. Hearts.
> Mine and yours. Yeah, all of you.
> The times we've given it away

for chump change.
The heart, the fist. If you're lucky
someone grabs your shoulder.

— and the grievously immoral behavior not of the author, whose macho exterior covers an androgynous sensitivity, but of his older brothers.

Dedicated to James Baldwin, Part II, "Time, Temperature," views racism in Detroit through personal and family history, from a prejudiced grandfather fixing black kids' bikes to the poet's open-mindedness. Part III, "Digger's Territory," is an Autobiography of Every(working)man, excoriation of the alienation of factory work and of repression by the Catholic Church, plus a vivid depiction of the alcoholic landscape into which workers escape. Part IV, "Trouble at the Drive-In," lashes out at the managerial class for causing the working class to turn its anger and frustration on itself:

and we're all kicking each other's asses
while the bosses are safe and dry
in Grosse Pointe or West Bloomfield or wherever
the fuck they live, laughing at *The New Yorker* cartoons
and thinking Woody fucking Allen is a genius, let me
tell you, Clint ain't no genius, but I understand
his movies, and I understand what's going on
up ahead, and I'm hearing sirens, and me and you,
we're in this together, buddy, just a couple dummies
like those two up there, and nobody's letting us in
and nobody's getting out, and it's only a matter of time
till somebody pulls a gun.

In these reactionary times of widespread disenfranchisement and AK-47s, the gun is likely to go off into the face of some black, some unemployed factory hand, some woman or ex-lover. The University of Pittsburgh Press is no *New Masses*, which more than threescore years ago Joseph Kalar called "the voice of low-brow failure" to distinguish it from *The New Republic* and *The Nation*, the "clean white pants of respectability." As Kalar described fitful sleep in his poem "Proletarian Night," through the dual consciousness of work and dream the committed poet naturally expresses the binding, anti-establishment values of freedom and justice:

> Though the body cries out for rest, writhing
> with aching flesh throughout the night,
> and sleep descends with rags that dull,
> conviction, still inviolate, remains,
> that sleep will not hail victory in,
> remove the steel thumbs of the mill
> that gouge into the temples (here and here),
> return one beam of lost, forgotten day,
> or drive one foe into the avenging street.

That Daniels turns to Clint Eastwood films for class identity shows to what extent human solidarity and social responsibility have been lost since artisanal labor disappeared at the turn of the century and political and economic reforms faded after World War II. We are worse off, and Jim Daniels' art reminds us why.

Susan Hahn's *Incontinence* — what Aristotle in his *Ethics* referred to as *akrasia* or "lack of self-control" — broadcasts autobiography as style, titles one poem "Hysterectomy as Metaphor," and in another asks:

> Who hears the mute
> clamor, the breaking of language
> into the oblivion? Who can pull
> the splinters out of the tongue
> and attend to our quick
> futures? What is really being
> written here?

If the author could have her wish, would she dissolve into her poem? In a sense she *has*, for she invites us to

> Enter my house
> as if it were my body, . . .

An unloved woman is like an uninked page: "the ache from the wait between" accompanies "the dream of rhythms that can't be held" and "the race to command impossible stanzas." Poem and poet are one both in text and context. This leads to the conceit of lovers as heavenly bodies and to the double meaning of titles like "Oral Interpretation" —

> I haven't gotten deep enough
> for words yet,

> and if I talk you'll recognize
> the old stubborn child noise —
> that constant thrashing
> against the palate
> as if it were every bolted door.
> Someday you'll hear me, free.
> Touching you, my voice
> will be exactly what I say.

Behind the facade of double sounds and other verbal formalities lie the facts of unhappiness — the dead husband, the lost lover, the murderous car crash, the suicide of love's ending, the oxymorons of experience —

> lift me off the hook of this
> life and let me go into the silence
> that is now your voice.

Particularly well-placed in the collection is the title poem, gathering the book's sub-themes into the overarching metaphor of the incontinence of love, which "gushed out of me too cloudy." The very "accident," as children call it, leads to salvation by water, rebirth into the spirit world:

> The sea seemed
> the only safe place
> to let go
> and live again —
> a return to where
> it all began, before
> the urgency and burn
> of anything human.

An editor at *TriQuarterly*, Susan Hahn is skillfully self-conscious — perhaps *too* self-conscious, perhaps too ready to ask a reader's indulgence in her anguish. To join the ecstasy and the pain of loving — the emotion and meaning — is extremely difficult, as Whitman's capacious celebrations show us in the great space they require in both our heads and hearts (as well as many lines on the page) and Dante shows in the fifth canto of *The Inferno* by witnessing Paolo and Francesca's story. Hahn has achieved something contemporary in her own way, a tribute to her deep sense of reality and to her ever-living idealism. She reveals a sense of beauty reaching far beyond the beach and the boudoir into the subtexts of poetry itself and, by patient seriousness, making the sexual passionately — or, better, lovingly — sensual. In her poems, her catastrophes, too, carry their dignity with them.

Brenda Hillman presents herself as an interlocutor between nature and the reader. The reader's friend, she is a born observer:

> This world is my twin
> but I was not cut from the same cloth, I passed
> through the shadow so I could be
> amazed at it —

The naïveté is charming and deceptive: "What mystery is inside a thing!" Her childlike eyes are big and round, but, like a child, she terrorizes herself with her own interior spaces. Having a marginal function in contemporary American society, a poet may be tempted to play variations of other roles, often exploiting or manipulating a sexual stereotype. *Iron John* is an example of self-inflation to the point of absurdity. Surely "the earth is feminine," as Hillman says and as the Egyptians said first, but how feminine I am not sure. "March Dawn," in which a child become a mother remembers being beaten by her clinging mother, is a composite of Hillman's interlocking dualism according to which the purpose or motivation for her poetry is expressed as a sort of program for consciousness and the emotion that drives it is the poetic texture, or passion, the two together offering a perception that moves back and forth, in and out, over itself:

> See your shadow in the dark — still gray grass,
> some radiance above it:
>
> everything has a border doesn't it?
> the edge where light cannot get in
>
> until joy knows the original wound.
>
> Which is why the earth is feminine,
> and the body, not the soul, cries out in heaven —

Primary experience of reality follows from the earth's ineluctable fruitfulness —

Plum blossoms everywhere!
. . . .

> then you knew for the bird as for you the world
> split open was stunningly beautiful
> though being alive was nearly impossible —

As a pendulum counts time on its swing from apogee to apogee, so a man or woman ticks off his or her life on an arc from pain to ecstasy and back. Ability to believe maintains momentum; each act of belief, itself an acknowledgment of a gift, strengthens the movement, which, like the simple perception of beauty, begins by discriminating among beautiful forms — seeing things in their colorful singularities against the background of universal shadowy gray. Trapped in the prison-house of its own emotions between anguished pessimism and buoyant passion, the self bounces between ancient and contemporary images, between formal and colloquial diction, but always comes round to what it most longs for — the ultimate freedom of love. As given in poems like "Holding On" and "The Hair," that love is humanly diminished by bourgeois self-consciousness. The perceptions are acute, but nothing can overcome aloneness in contemporary middle-class America, especially the declaration that it has been overcome:

> whatever I have loaned
> has been given back to me, the body
> inside the soul
> he holds, is held by, and is not lonely —

To compare it to the Joy expressed in The Song of Solomon or to the grand ebullience of Siva's love-making with Parvati in the Sanskrit epic *The Origin of the Young God* (never mind what has happened to the Romantic tradition) is to see how small in the nuclear world of war and violence the world of love has become and how valiantly and forcefully a strong poet struggles to push the boundaries back.

> But of the suffering inherent in matter,
> what shall we say?

Hard to know. The sardonic "Useful Shadow," a culmination of the "traveler" and "shadow" poems, bites back at the hypocrisies of superficial practicality and yet longs for purposeful dedication:

Handsome nothing
standing at the heart of matter
with your self-hate and your twelve month contract:
no one was checking. Before
you'd done a single thing, you were enough —

Self imposes self on others, on the natural world. The terror of love
is its mortality. If only a person, a lover, could retain the remembered humility before the moment or be like the wintry seeds that

        stayed close to other seeds and
lived on vanishing,

once they had felt the presence of the others
they didn't need anything
they couldn't add to their existence, in any way —

   It's a sign of John Updike's urbanity that among his poems of forty
years are many that walk the line between being and non-being.
They insist on bringing into existence feelings, at least, if not things,
that might otherwise seem to be discards. What the proper middle
class would cover up he determinedly, even enthusiastically, with
child-like wonder, lays bare, as in "My Children at the Dump":

To me, too, the waste seems wonderful.
Sheer hills of television tubes, pale lakes
of excelsior, landslides
of perfectly carved carpentry-scraps,
sparkplugs like nuggets. . . .
. . . .

        I came to add
my fragments to this universe of loss,
purging my house, ridding a life
no longer shared of remnants.
My daughter brings a naked armless doll,
still hopeful in its dirty weathered eyes,
and I can only tell her, "Love it now.
Love it now, but we can't take it home."

The emotional directness and the autobiographical simplicity only
partly mask the sophisticated irony of the last line.

That poem dates from the early Sixties. A poem from the Nineties, using some of the same vocabulary—"universe," "house"—and underlying concept of male/female sexuality is "Mouse Sex," in which the poet supposes that a dead, fat mouse is pregnant, discovers a "pumpkin-seed-shaped break in the dulcet fur," and recalls making love in "another woods-surrounded house" when an unexpected sound "turned my erection inconvenient" but soon, in the following quiet, the woman said, "Put it in me," revealing what the poet had not expected—namely, that sex has an equitable basis:

> The cat creeps below, but lady mice
> still put their dulcet selves at risk, and die.
> . . . .
>
> Suspended above the abyss of her desire,
> I feel as far-flung as a constellation.
> Colors: the golden-edged trees, the lilac sheets,
> the mousy green of her self-startled eyes.
> We are furtive, gigantic, our stolen hour
> together a swollen eternity.
> We enter into one another; the universe
> rises about us like a hostile house.

Some of the distancing comes from age and the sweet indifference to false propriety that results from accumulated experience and the sense that time is running out, but some also comes from greater confidence in the power of words to name not names but emotions and to find comfort, if not identity itself, in separateness and solitude. One's pain is not more pleasant, but one can more skillfully, because wisely, accommodate one's losses. One can play on both sides—or, despite Aristotle's laws of logic, one can be both A and not-A, and to hell with the law of the excluded middle. In fact, one swings back and forth between the apogees of self and not-self, entering into each other hotly even as the rest of the world coldly turns away.

The everyday world as captured in Updike's elegant, urbane prose, which for years has captivated readers and critics from Manhattan to Moscow, a distinct "product" of the Fifties but perdurable beyond those stuffed-shirt years, rises from his poetry with greater emotional investment. Who knows whether there is more autobiographical "truth" in *The Centaur*, a novel about his father and himself as son, or in "Back Bay," a poem about about his son and himself as father, but the compaction of the poem and the swiftness of its delivery give it a lyric plausibility and tolerate a metaphoric generalization, which show that the author knows how big and how old the really complex real world is. Having gone clothes shopping with his son and remembered a woman he once knew, the poet concludes:

> The bright streets struck us again, and I looked
> for her, unable to grasp how gone she was
> from this panorama, how she had existed,
> as the living still did, less a thing
> than as a pattern or shimmer in what was seen
> for a season or two, a ripple in water
> that catches light, then spills it like a pod.

The elegance of that mind in the simplicity of its perceptions breeds a unique power. The language, like a lacewing, is both there and not there, eminently visible and quite beautiful but at the same time so light, so independent, so deliberately transitory that it simultaneously persuades us of its truthfulness and yet makes no literal impression. It handles its subject completely without marring or mauling. It tells us all we need to know — all that is knowable about the subject as individual and as design — while acknowledging the delicacy of creative work and not leaning its elbows on it at all. Like all of Updike's fine poems, it's a trip round ourselves on an island of time, always coming back to where we are.

Although invented in the late eighteenth century as a way of getting around the inflexibility of syllabic French versification, by the end of the nineteenth century the prose poem had become a means of expressing originality. Prose poems have been anthologized for a hundred years and written about by German, French, English, and American critics for more than sixty. Now there is a magazine called *The Prose Poem: an International Journal*, but, as the subtitle of C. H. Ford' s A *Little Anthology of the Poem In Prose* warns, we must look out for the "possibilities and impossibilities of the prose poem: junk, jargon, and a few gems." Jay Meek's new, fifth book of gems, *Windows*, builds a house of meaning out of three floors each of a dozen rooms, each room with a window looking out on the so-called real world and inviting us to discover an inner reality made up of time and imagination, that recombinant memory in which, even short of Hell, lies the substance of our being:

SHADOWLAND

> This is the word I remembered because it called to me. This is what I have kept. . . . But one summer, after forty years, I went back to my childhood home. . . . I felt the years fall from me. . . . Overhead, on a monitor, a musical comedy was playing. In it, the dancers came and went like breath on a glass, and the ensemble of children who danced with them, instead of making the shop more real and lasting, gave it a flickering beauty, as if our town and everyone who held it dear had been breathed into being. When mother died, father went into the dark, where a great curtain parted: fiddlers played, the credits rolled, and the angels threw up their hands with nonchalant forgiveness and an almost frivolous despair.

Like all good art and all competent philosophy, it is a poetry that begins at the beginning:

> How much life I spend in consciousness alone, mapping the joys I see: this fountain, a few iron chairs, shadows of things. These touch me, wonderfully, and go on.
>
> ("Medici Fountain")

On to what? On to form. "*Ostranenie!*" shouted the Formalists. "Defamiliarize!" Indeed, that is what aesthetic form does. As Bakhtin pointed out, it liberates content from context: "The word ceases . . . to desire something of the real beyond its borders." Changing direction well beyond the Formalists, Bakhtin came to understand the primacy of the artist's ethical role, that is, how the artist's personality as form was expressed through the personal responsibility of creating a second consciousness in the artwork. For Bakhtin, as Gary Saul Morson writes in *Mikhail Bakhtin: Creation of a Prosaics*, the aesthetic achievement lay in non-systematic functioning, that is, in "the radical singularity of the artist who transferred ethical responsibility from the content onto his own person by means of an active application of form."

Without distancing, the artwork has no figure of its own to create shape in the mind. Without the transformation of content, it has no cognitive value. If we put a Meek prose poem such as "Shadowland" or "Sudden Appearances" or "Rude Bathers" beside, say, Charles Simic's "Theseus and Ariadne" or David Antin's "remembering recording representing" or Russell Edson's "The Marionettes of Distant Masters," we see how the power of form in Meek's work expresses the presence of consciousness creating the reality of human space. In part, it is a question of seriousness — Antin is not only silly but also insubstantial; insubstantial silliness is soon wearying — but fundamentally it is a question of illumination: to what extent does the light within the poem shining along the path on the poet's quest to turn feeling into knowledge light up the reader's mind? Working on everything around us, memory electrifies the imagination, which, through the idiosyncratic application of form, creates the achieved content. Looking back to the past and ahead to the future through the window of a poem, the mind that remembers becomes — is — the substance of what we know.

> Perhaps one day, entering a tramontane village, we might find all that's lost to us, forms sheered off from their substances — sollerets and phaetons and mortsafes — still without rust in the rarified air. Who can say? I have seen pictures of a man who carried inside him the incomplete body of his twin, only the spine and shoulders visible on his chest as if his brother had dived into him. In the whole of the universe, who's to say the human form is right? Truly, we are capable of infinite variation, like the ocean our crossing takes small measure of, the whitecaps falling on one another like shadows of the possible world.
> ("The Beautiful and Invisible Tree That Rises Through the Universe for Which the Stars Are Leaves")

Idealistic and original, this poetry turns the self inside out, like a glove, and refits it to the world's hand. Personal becomes Universal. Casual diction, non-metrical and intellectual unconventionality, and patient introspection — the careful combing of the past — draw us inevitably closer to the ever-present but elusive mystery of "the possible world."

"Make it new!" cried Pound, cobbled The Cantos together, and lashed the world into Imagism, The Waste Land, and modern poetry. "Stand up now like a man!" the Lord barked at Job. Meek does. Refracting our time in elegant simplicity and fidelity, with affection and full ethical responsibility, his life-sized poetry shows how to make it new — and newer.